MONSTER'S CHILDREN

THE TRICKSTERS' WAR: I

DANIEL HANSEN

Daniel Hansen

Steve,

You will always be
the love of my life
thanks for all the
good times

[signature]

DEDICATION

I dedicate this book to those that put up with me

Daniel Hansen

CONTENTS

GIRL WITH A SMILE

Jamie smiled at the man before her. She was not happy with him. She was not happy at all, but a smile calmed people. People liked smiles. No matter what she felt inside, the smile made her seem more likeable. At least that is what she had heard. If you wanted to be liked and accepted, well, then you needed to learn to smile.

The man seemed to live on some private island, where a Pandora station played that only he could hear. He was just one of those people. Self-possessed and walking through life with their own theme music. You could almost see his head nod to the tune. Jamie had no idea why he had knocked on her door or what it meant that he was here. So she smiled as she had taught herself to do, and he smiled back. Two fake smiles to comfort and calm people who required neither comfort nor calm.

Jamie was six feet tall, which she hoped meant she was almost grown. She already towered over most of the other girls in her school and not a few adults. It was a constant hassle to be so tall. A thing for people to notice about someone who wanted not to be noticed. She was taller than the man in the brown tweed jacket, untucked button-up blue shirt, and jeans who hopped in his own private music video called her door. He was average height and had a wiry, athletic frame. Although he was so much shorter than she was, he seemed bigger than life, bigger than she was. He had a presence that seemed to fill the moment. It drew her in, willing her to try and live within the movie in which his soundtrack ruled.

The man before her stood in the door like a cop, but he did not seem like a cop. For one thing, tight around his neck he had a strange thick, green necklace that was much too flamboyant to be professional. His demeanor said that he was in authority, yet everything about him said he was a lie. Not that he was telling a lie, but that everything he was... well, lied. Jamie's father was behind her somewhere in the apartment, most likely drinking a beer and watching TV, and here was this stranger, smiling away at her. Smiling at her with the same practiced smile she used on others.

He was a mid- to late-twenty-something white guy,

average height, athletic build, with long blonde hair and blue eyes that burned in his face. His clothing and stance looked like those of every other white guy Jamie had ever seen in government-issued authority but with no real power. Those eyes of his told another story; they screamed predator. They were dead and excitingly alive all at the same time, as if a fire burned out from his handsome face. A handsome face that was set in a bored and worn smile, but the eyes studied her face and the apartment behind her with a fanatic's stare. A fanatic who didn't care about anything but was still curious. She saw her own monster in those eyes.

"Ma'am, your papa home?" He smiled back at her smile, and she had the odd feeling that his was better than hers, so she upped the ante and smiled back harder.

"What the hell's a papa?"

"Look, Jamie, just get your dad. We need to talk."

The man's tone brooked no backtalk, and his smile slipped away into what appeared to be a practiced frown. Jamie realized that she would need to start practicing her frowns. He sounded upset and bored all at the same time. He went from languishingly happy to fiercely demanding, all in the blink of an eye. She saw what he was attempting to portray—the standard put-upon public servant dealing with an obstinate teen. And yet Jamie could see the truth in his eyes, still uncaring, still searching.

What worried her, though, was why he was here. He obviously knew her name, so he was here about her. The last thing she needed was more outside authority figures coming to her home and upsetting her parents. She had been careful lately; there was no way he could be here about any of her more recent adventures. And yet she could see no path around allowing this man in the doorway to speak to her father.

As she turned and pointed into the apartment, his frown switched quickly back to a smile. She walked towards her father and felt the man follow behind. Without looking around, she knew he studied every minuscule detail of her home. He filed her life away in the few minutes it took to get to the living room.

The apartment was a standard lower-middle-class home in Chicago. The photos on the walls were of her family and their friends. Her mother smiled out at her over the heads of Jamie's siblings in most of the pictures, and her father stood looking stern and stoic beside his wife. The whole room was a mix of brown and tan with a few yellow and red splashes thrown in. What her mother called autumn colors. Jamie knew it looked ragged on the edges, but a certain sense of her mother's style shone through. As they walked down the hallway, she felt the man like a dancer at her back.

Her father sat on the couch, beer in hand and TV running. He was an older black man in a grey t-shirt and jeans with short, grey hair and a world-weary look on his face. For a moment, Jamie saw her father through the man's eyes. It was midday, and he had a beer in hand and a TV on. But she wondered if the man saw her father. There was an important difference between seeing someone and seeing someone; everyone wanted to be seen. Jamie wanted the stranger to see her father as she did. He was raising three children with a woman he loved. He worked hard, doing shifts at night for a boss he cared little about. But the company took good care of him, and he stayed with them despite his dreams, all to ensure that his family was fed.

His eldest daughter, Jamie, was more than a handful. She spent her entire life falling out of the lines that those around her had drawn on the page of life. She had been caught stealing and fighting more than she could recall, and her parents had missed work to talk to schools and law enforcement more than they could afford. Yet they continued to love her and care for her. They tried, and she knew they tried. Was any of that what the man saw when he looked at her father? Or was it just a black man having a beer in the middle of the day as he watched some lame sports event?

If her father was surprised by this unexpected visitor

coming into his home during the middle of the day, he did not show it, beyond a world-weary sigh as he leaned forward and looked at his daughter.

"What the hell did you do now, girl?"

"Oh, she did wondrous things, sir. Wondrous."

The odd turn of phrase seemed out of place to Jamie, yet her father walked over it like it had been lying down in the road. "I am talking to my daughter."

"And I am here to talk about your daughter." The man ignored her father's irritated look and just pushed through. He held out his hand with his put-upon smile, and Jamie wondered how her father could not see that it was merely a hollow expression on the man's face. How her father could be so close and not see the oddness. "Most folk call me Alex, my friend, and I am here because your wee childe applied to a very special school that she is uniquely qualified for. Uniquely qualified." The man's hand hung in front of her father, untouched. His tone and words said bumpkin excited to be in town.

"School? Special? What the hell did she do that was so special? Hasn't had a day in her life she hasn't gotten into some kind of trouble."

"Well, I must say we at the Kootenai Academy for the

Specialist of Special Children see great potential in this here girl. Potential, I tell ya. Potential. And we would like to discuss the possibility of her attending our institution. I do have brochures."

The two men looked at each other. One with his hand out, the other ignoring it. The conversation continued back and forth. Jamie was confused. She had never heard of this school for the Specialist of Children, let alone applied for it. What the hell was this guy talking about? Jamie was anything but a top student. She had always considered herself special but never in a way those in authority ever noticed, or that she would want them to notice. And yet here he was. Who would have taken notice of her like this?

"We will teach her to navigate without ever showing her a road. I am telling you—look at this brochure."

Jamie looked at him again. He was still in his brown tweed jacket. He still had his uncaring, burning eyes. But he seemed more present, more there than anything else in the room. His soundtrack had come with him, and it was filling the entire apartment. He never dropped his hand, yet it did not seem he was being snubbed. Instead, it felt as if a natural weight sat upon him. A wait her father had just not yet reached the end of. She heard her father's anger and decided to start paying attention again.

"Look, peckerwood, I do not know what you and your sick pervert school want with my little girl, but you can take your dumb ass and get out of..."

Jamie's heart jumped as Alex turned to her and looked only at her. This man saw her. Everything slowed; the world stopped; her father's tirade passed over and through them as if it came from a turned-down music player. Her father was in a different world from them. Everything was in a different world from them. And the man who looked at her was not the man at her door or the man talking to her father. Alex's look was focused only on her. The world was within that focus. Everything else was them, and this moment—this confrontation—was them. He was waiting for her, looking at her. Seeing her. Waiting and looking in a way no one had waited or looked before.

"Jamie, this group will have people of many races. Will that be an issue? It appears your father seems to care."

"What? No, but..."

The man who looked at her now had no smile. He had no frown. He just was. He had nothing about him that was fake. Well, except that the clothing he wore was nothing more than a simple costume. It did not fit him, somehow, yet every piece looked perfectly tailor-made just for him. The eyes that looked at her held no kindness, no cruelty—only curiosity. His voice was steady and calm.

"Jamie, this is your chance. I see it in you. I know you. I know the impulses you give in to, and the trouble you have made. The thefts, the violence, the joy you have taken in whims you cannot explain. I am here to offer you a life where you can indulge those impulses. Embrace them. Learn to become the greatest thing your potential portents. Do you want that?"

Jamie wondered if this asshole was joking. She could see his eyes and saw no humor, only the same serious curiosity he had switched to. Her father's words kept rolling out as Jamie and Alex spoke. On some vague level, she knew that what her father said did not matter. Her answer to Alex was all that mattered. Somehow, he would change her father's mind for her if she said yes, and he would walk away if she said no. She saw it in his eyes, the simple unforgiving curiosity. And she felt the truth of his offer inside her. The truth to let go of the shell she had carried for so long.

"What does that mean? What would I do?"

"Yes or no: do you wish to go where you can learn to be what you feel inside?"

"Yes, but..."

"Go pack a bag."

There was no other discussion in the man's eyes. Jamie had chosen, and he was ready to move forward. The man turned to her father, and it was as if the conversation between them had been ongoing. It was as if Jamie had imagined the whole conversation between herself and Alex. Her father and the stranger had merely continued their talk in this, the real world. Her father was no longer as angry; Alex was still seductive; the two men still talked; her father held a brochure.

The moment outside of time they had shared was impossible. And yet Jamie turned without thinking to go pack. Alone in her room, she smiled.

******

Jamie had gotten in a taxi with the stranger and left the only home she had ever known. They had traveled on a plane together for most of the day, and yet, she had learned little about him, other than that he rolled his own cigarettes and smoked at every chance he got. Usually with a glass of alcohol in his other hand. He rarely talked unless speaking seemed to serve some purpose. She watched him go through several conversations with flight attendants and people in airports; he matched accents and colloquialisms with everyone he talked with. And at some point, he had traded the tweed jacket and button-up shirt for a hoodie and ball cap.

He barely spoke to Jamie, except in one long-winded tirade at a restaurant in Denver during their layover. Alex had recited all the reasons he had chosen the place and why their food was so amazing. He talked ingredients and fusions, and Jamie silently listened, shocked after his long silence. He was like a food critic and guide all at once, discussing flavor choices and mouth feels of the tacos he had ordered them. It seemed a practiced speech that did not require her input, which was lucky, seeing as she had little idea what he was going on about.

Jamie had hoped Alex would become less of a stranger on the trip, yet he only got stranger. He danced from one personality to another, becoming someone new with each person who approached them. A constant stream of people materialized on his face, but in his eyes, she saw the same theme song playing nonstop. Inside, somewhere deep, he was looking out, even as his outsides changed to match everyone else.

Alex never answered her questions. He never reacted to what she said or did. She was the one person on the trip who did not get the big sell. It was frustrating for her. All her life, she had prided herself on being able to cause a reaction. In parents, in teachers, in her friends, and especially on the male side of the equation. But he did not react. She tried to be friendly, then flirty, then aggravating, but nothing caused even a glimmer in his eye. He had no reaction; he was neither interested nor annoyed with her. Just a complete feeling of indifference. Jamie could not understand his indifference, and it built a pressure in her mind, making her tense.

She started to wonder if she had made a mistake. She did not miss her family. The goodbyes had been tear-stained on her mother's part. Somehow, while she packed, her father had gone from angered refusal to pride in his daughter's achievement of being accepted and the new "wonderful" opportunity the school provided. And yet, for all the brochures and sweet words Alex had used, Jamie had learned neither his last name nor anything real about the school, other than that it was in Idaho, somewhere a few hours south of the Canadian border. What they taught or why the students were so special she never could pin down. Every question had received a non-answer that danced around solid facts. But they were special, and she was special. Had to be true: her mother had said it several times. So no, she did not miss her family, but she wondered what exactly she had become a part of.

The last leg of the trip covered large tracts of forests and mountains before going over a large lake and medium-sized city. Trees and plants covered the land beneath her like a thick, green blanket of sharply poking-up branches pushing against the deep green-blue lake that sparkled in the sunshine. The jagged peaks of rock and dirt that clawed their way through the mass of green only accentuated the wild and beautiful nature of what lay beneath her.

Even the cities and towns they passed over were part of the natural landscape, like meadows in the forests. The low buildings and many natural areas within the towns helped create this effect. When they finally passed over the city which would be her new home, the sheer number of parks and trees made the city seem as though it were built into the forests, rather than carved out of them. It was breathtaking. The natural beauty of the land beneath her was a shock, after her years living in the metropolis of Chicago. She was amazed that so much green could exist in the world, after the drab greys of the windy city. It was breathtaking, and for a moment, she felt ready to embrace the new life she had chosen.

The small plane they took on the final leg of the trip touched down in a small, dirty airport that looked like it was never used, except by small local pilots. The jerking and jumping of the small plane made Jamie's stomach hurt and her eyes water. How could people do this regularly, this jarring insanity of travel? The elevation had not bothered her, just this nasty hump to hump every time they hit some turbulence. Her stomach would roll around in nauseated swirls, broken up by quick trips of the stomach slamming into her throat and then back down. Jamie was not a fan of air travel, it seemed.

After touchdown, Alex briskly walked her from the metal stair car to the end of the tarmac to grab her luggage. The small airport was encircled by a chain link fence that looked like it had not been maintained in fifty years. Jamie was shocked at how small the airport was. How houses and fields of wheat seemed to push right up against the fence between it and the city. She did not have much time, though, to really look around.

Alex loaded her into a dark-colored Lexus that was sitting in the parking lot. The car was comfortable and warm; it was likely the nicest car Jamie had ever been in. It had a central heads-up display and leather seats framed in what looked like polished wood and chrome. She could feel the air coming in from the seat, ensuring she was neither too warm nor too cold. If Alex was proud of the car, he did not show it. Nor did he inform her of where they were going and what they were doing. He merely held open the door, waited for her to get in, then got in himself and started to drive. Now that they were alone, the silent non-answering Alex was here. He could have at least whistled, Jamie thought; it would have made him seem more human.

They drove about an hour down a long, four-lane highway

packed with a surprising number of cars for such a small city, before crossing through a downtown touristy cavalcade of shops and restaurants. They drove back out of the touristy area into a run-down section of broken buildings and tired homes before exiting into trees and wilderness. They kept driving, deep into a wilderness wilder then anything Jamie had thought possible.

She read one sign that pointed the way to a Lake Fernan, but Alex neither slowed nor turned. Instead, he drove up and up, into a deeper and darker forest. They passed through large, open areas, and at a few points, Jamie had to hold her breath as the road became single-lane dirt with large, broken rocks and scraggly brush on one side and a sheer drop to nothing on the other. She had never seen such beauty and grandeur that seemed completely untouched by human hands. The car jerked toward the edge, and she squeaked, grabbing at the dash.

They finally reached their destination. It was a large, ancient-looking stone building surrounded by cut grass and out-buildings, but more importantly, surrounded by trees. The out-buildings ranged from other stone works to glass, brick, and wood. They seemed a hodgepodge of building materials, and yet all were crafted to fit into the overall feel of the place. The style was either intimidating-fortress-of-rich-evil-mastermind-bent-on-world-domination, or high-end-boarding-school-for-children-of-wealth-and-power. Jamie guessed, in the end, they were all the same style. They were high up a mountain; that is all she knew. And it was beautiful, like something from a storybook. She just stared out the window for a minute, taking it all in. Breathing it all in. This was her new home.

Alex jumped out of the car and breathed deep. He held open Jamie's door until she got out. Without a word, he popped the trunk and started walking toward the large front entrance. He did not turn to her or utter a word, just walked up the stairs and toward the massive double doors.

"Don't bother to help a lady," Jamie said under her breath, in response to which she heard a slight, quick laugh from Alex as he sauntered away. Well, at least she had finally gotten a reaction.

The walls of the main building were stone—large chunks laid long enough ago that plants climbed up the sides, all the way to the roof. The stone looked as though it were made of whole chunks fit together as they were found, rather than hewn blocks. It gave the impression of a mishmash of lines snaking across the wall, as though a hammer had cracked a solid surface or a spider web was inlaid in the wall. The doors were of a heavy, dark wood that gleamed against the grey-blue stone. Alex pushed both doors open as Jamie struggled with her luggage behind him.

Again, she heard him breathe a sigh that sounded like relief.

Inside was a riot of simplicity. The shining hardwood floor extended back into a room large enough for a basketball court. The floor was polished to the point that she could almost see her reflection in the wood. Stairwells and doorways meandered away from the main room, randomly situated along the walls and alcoves. None of it seemed planned or predictable in its nature. Yet Jamie had the impression that it was likely the most solidly built structure she had ever seen. So much work for something so huge, so complex, so well-built, and yet it followed no real design that she could see. It looked as if the builder had felt like adding an alcove here and a stairway here, so there they were. Why use symmetry or plan it out when you could wing it?

It was not the size of the room (She wondered if she should call it a hall, maybe.) that immediately caught her attention but the four teens in the middle of the room. They were all dressed in tight-fitting red-and-black clothing and seemed to be performing a series of matching movements. It was an exercise routine, Jamie guessed, and she had a feeling it was some kind of martial art. Their moves were a fluid dance from one formation to another in a smooth, unbroken motion. The teens were each and every one beautiful in motion and beautiful in form. Jamie could not help but feel a silent stab of jealousy.

These were classmates of hers? It was unfair that they would be so attractive and graceful.

Of the four, two were male and two were female. All of them had longish hair. They seemed to all be of a similar age to Jamie. And again, she was irked to see that they were all in better shape, and from the look of it, more agile. Strong, thin, athletic builds coupled with the fresh feeling that teens emanate. Jamie knew she was strong, but her body erred on the side of gangly, more than athletic, in her eyes. She was also aware that she had lost a hint of her teen-ness as she pushed into adulthood. These kids would be stiff competition. Jamie understood that she would need to begin some hard lessons to compete with them.

Jamie had been surrounded by white and black kids for most of her life. She had never really cared, but society had made it clear that there was an "us" and "them" that usually unfolded along racial lines. That was how it had been taught in her house and in her school. It made it easy to find a group, and she had hoped that it would serve her here as a shortcut.

But not one of these kids was black, and only one, a young boy, was white. He had longish red, curly hair and freckles. He was medium height for a boy, but his height could likely be due to his age, or it could be that everyone seemed short to Jamie. He looked like he could bench press a small car, yet something about him screamed that he lifted for the look, not the ability. But in Jamie's normal dissection of group dynamics, he was alone. It seemed that unless there were other kids in this school, that standard shortcut to becoming part of the group was unopen to her here. She supposed she could use gender, but she was not sure. Other girls did not often like her.

What she did have to work with would be a challenge, using her old methods. One thin Asian girl was as short as the white boy. Jamie came to terms with the fact that these two were of average height and that she would be the tallest, at six feet, unless one of these people hit a growth spurt. But Jamie wanted to think of them as short, so she did. The Asian girl was beautiful in a way that made Jamie's stomach sink and tighten all at the same time. This was an alpha female who knew it. Worse, she had all the tools to keep her status out of the hands of an interloper like Jamie.

The other two teens were brown, which meant Jamie had no idea what their races were. The girl was a pretty little thing. She was likely a similar age to the rest, but the shortest of the group. She seemed cutely prim and yet dangerous all at once. A difficult mix to pull off. It was disturbing and exhilarating when done this well. Her lips were a bright red that drew the eye. The boy was younger-looking and yet taller than the other three. He had long, straight hair that hung loose on his shoulders and messily around his face. Unlike the white kid, he seemed to be thin in his athleticism. He was covered in muscle, but none of it bulged. He kept looking at Jamie and then the rest as if unsure if he liked the new addition to their group. Something nervous and twitchy filled his complete stillness.

They all stopped in the middle of their sparring and ran over to stand before Alex and Jamie. They did not quite stand at attention, but they also were not as relaxed as teens on a street corner would be. Alex looked each of them over, glancing up and down, inspecting them. His eyes took in every detail, and the intense scrutiny Jamie had felt at her apartment returned to his eyes. What did she see there under the scrutiny? Was it pride or disappointment? Jamie noticed that each of them wore a thick necklace that matched Alex's, but each was made of different materials. All of the necklaces were tight around their necks.

"My children, this is Jamie, our newest recruit. She will need to be shown around and informed of the basics. Nettle, she'll need to see her room." He looked at the Asian girl as he said this. If the girl's beauty and tight clothing affected him, there was no indication. Instead, he seemed to be speaking to a servant barely in need of acknowledgment. Jamie was comforted for a moment. Well, at least she was not the only one who caused no reaction. To him, they were all equally unworthy of attention. Alex turned back to Jamie. "Jamie, this is Nettle, followed by Joe, María, and Russ. Please get your things situated, get cleaned up. Dinner will be ready soon."

Alex seemed to have dismissed her, and for a second, Jamie was unsure of what to do next, where to go. A moment of not wanting to lose the one person she knew here overtook her. This strange building, this new home, all that had happened. She did not want to be alone with these new people just yet. "What would you like me to do?"

"Why would I care?"

With that, Alex turned and walked away. The discussion was over; that was clear. He was done with her for now. His dismissal should have hurt, she suspected, but it did not. It invigorated her to be here. To know she was on her own. His dismissal cut loose the ties that had bound her to the man, ties that no longer held her. Where others might have felt bereft or snubbed, Jamie felt liberated. Alex was done with her, so she had no need to hold on to him. Of course, the transaction might have weakened her in front of the other students. She dreaded to think how they had taken her question. Hopefully, they did not see it as pleading. As weakness. She would need to limit that loss of face. She needed to ensure they had not seen it as needy.

Jamie looked at the small class. Nettle was the Asian girl's name, apparently. Jamie knew she should connect the girl to a specific type of Asian, but really, she did not know any better. There were so many, and Jamie had no idea what was what. She made a mental note to use her confusion in a joke later. She would never tell Nettle that she couldn't tell what type of Asian she was. People could be picky about such things, and the last thing Jamie wanted was to upset the beautiful girl. Joe turned out to be a Native American kid, and María was Latina. It was nice when people self-branded. That meant the white kid was Russ. María's accent placed her from another country south of the border, and Joe sounded Canadian. Both made sense, in Jamie's limited understanding of the two groups they hailed from. A Latina who was likely Mexican and a Native who was Canadian. Nettle and Russ, though, came across as good old Americans, by the sounds of them. Jamie wondered why Nettle did not have an accent and then wondered if that was racist. Maybe Alex's original worry had been correct. Maybe she was racist.

She did not know; maybe they were all American, or maybe they could all be foreigners. Not that Jamie cared. Why would she? What had countries done for her? Not a damn thing. Their races—other than the oddity of them all being different— really mattered little to her, as well. She was practiced in labeling people through the medium of nationality because of how she had been raised. But it was lazy and seemed to be unhelpful here. She thought that if she was racist, it was because she had just been too lazy to try and meet other people and form groups. She was realizing she might need a new system of boxing up her new little society. Their races and places of origin did not worry her.

Her one worry was that they all seemed younger and more athletic. Not to mention they all exuded confidence and beauty in ways few people she had ever met did. She knew her own beauty, but she could not help but measure herself against them. She was attractive, she knew, but not at their level. Beauty was an important tool in this world. Jamie was not pleased.

These students had been here first, knew the rules, and could possibly be potential competitors. She would need to catch up with them on the athletic side—not to mention the fact that she still did not know what they would be studying. She would need to find out the currency of popularity here and begin collecting it. It was a constant drill Jamie ran through her head when meeting new people. Assign who was who. Who she could use. And who was competition. Work her way toward enjoying the benefits of a group for as long as she could stand them.

She realized she had four sets of eyes looking at her in the same way she was looking at them. They were assigning her a value. This was new. They were fitting her into the group dynamic. Testing mental hypotheses of how best to use her. The wheels of social manipulation were turning for them all. She could see it. She could understand it. She realized she would have to play harder to become the best. It was not a thing she was used to. She began to understand why people found her so unnerving. She felt the stirring of adrenalin in her system as fight or flight kicked in.

She smiled. She had made the right choice. This was her new family.

SETTLING IN

Nettle liked to talk. She smoked like a chimney and rattled off facts like they were old girlfriends. Jamie slowly unpacked while Nettle monotoned through idle thoughts she believed Jamie should know. Nettle lounged on the bed that was soon to be Jamie's, looking like any other flighty sex kitten ready to gossip. It was weird. Jamie had not had many friends in the past and even fewer female friends. She had never imagined that her potential friend would be this person in front of her. Nettle was gorgeous in both dress and mannerism. She exuded seduction. Like one of those old Hollywood starlets who Jamie's mother loved to watch, Nettle breathed out lustful thoughts and breathed in seduction. If it had been Jamie on the bed, she would have looked like a gangly house cat trying to eat its own tail. All lumps and bumps that looked appealing due to her being comfortable and little else. Yet there was Nettle, like a wild tiger, stretched out in a way that would have drawn anyone's eyes to all the places she wanted them drawn. She effortlessly accentuated those places in ways that would have made the Pope need to hold a Bible in front of himself.

Further, Nettle gave off the air of being flighty and jumped from one topic to the other. She chimed in about things while Jamie was unpacking. She dragged in a smoke then went off on the inability to get a good drink on property since Hempel kept everything on lockdown. All in all, her speech was like a whirlwind that served the purpose of drawing one's eyes to the girl. It was background noise that Jamie had tuned out while she unpacked. A steady burbling stream that just kept running in a calming and peaceful fashion that Jamie found she enjoyed. Nettle was interesting, in a way Jamie could not place. And for all the differences they had, Jamie felt a kinship with the girl that she had not felt with many people before her. She had never imagined finding friendship in someone like this, but there seemed to be a closeness forming. Just to be sure Nettle felt a connection as well, Jamie turned to Nettle and smiled her smile and tuned back into what the girl was saying.

"Chicago, huh? Sounds windy and cold, like here in winter. Cold" Nettle scrunched up her face and shivered in a way that made a dramatic point about cold. "Alex found me in Honolulu. Not cold there. Hot and blossoming. I was boosting cars to race and then ditch. I tried to boost his car. A beautiful little Jag. Fell right into his trap, and he took me home. Knew right where I lived without even asking. I thought he was some weirdo pervo cop-stalker, or something. But he just ignored my questions and strolled right in. I thought for sure, here it comes. I am going to jail, and the parents are going to hate me. But instead, he promised my parents I was going to a school for gifted youngsters. How silly is that? Promised them I would graduate from a top prep school and get into an amazing college. They ate it up. I was eleven. I had no idea what was going on. Been here the longest. I was the first." She said it with a finality and a surety that for her, "first" meant not only in time but in ranking. Nettle was very much the alpha in the group. She only needed subtle hints to indicate it, yet she seemed to like the flat statement of fact. She marked her territory well. Jamie was surprised—years Nettle had been here.

"Russ came in from Seattle about two years ago. Parents gone, we think." Her shrugged shoulders and the flip of her smoke implied nobody really cared. "Alex found him living on the streets, stealing wallets. No parents around. He promised Russ food and a place to live. God, for all Russ knew, Alex could have been planning to pimp him out." Her tone said that Russ should have asked for more than food and a roof, if that was going to be his fate.

"He found María down in Mexico City about a month after Russ. Some rich 'connected' family." Nettle rolled her eyes and smiled. "And she won't let us forget it, even if she is just a kid. 'They are connected.'" Nettle did her best at a Spanish accent that was close but still an utter failure. Mostly it just sounded racist. "Not sure what he told her family, but they signed on that dotted line. María said they did not even bother to tell their princess anything but to go pack. I guess there was a row when he walked in and an ass-kissing goodbye when they walked out. From the sounds of it, they all but carried her to his car. I guess having a crime lord family is not always a great thing.

"Joe—well, he is the baby of the group, from some tribe up in Canada. Just got here about seven months back. Alex went in dressed as a priest, I guess, to talk to Joe's family. There was some issue with whatever Joe was up to. He won't talk about it. Joe being all hush-hush, but what's important is Alex promised to save him. The parentals, I guess, thought it was worth a shot to save his soul." She giggled for a second, then stopped and sighed. "That kid, always trying to sell us on how spiritual he is 'cause he is 'in touch with the earth.'" Nettle made air quotes and giggled again. "But don't trust it. None of us are spiritual. How can we be? With what we are? Well, I mean, you know?" Her question was not a question any more than her attempt to seem like a silly, gossipy girl had reached her eyes in the conversation. It was a test—as serious as the person who hid deep down inside Nettle, covered by this flighty mask she wore so well. Jamie knew that this was the part she needed to pay attention to. The simpering, sexy looks and unimportant gossip were not the test. They were not why the girl had come to her room to interview her and gauge her value. This was the test and the real face of the girl she needed to impress.

"I know what?"

"You know—'special.'" Again, the air quotes made an appearance, and this time, Nettle laughed, a laugh that touched her big, dark eyes, but barely. Pretense was dripping slowly from the room, leaving bare two intense young women trying to communicate past the masks they so often wore for a world that could not appreciate them.

"What does make us special? I mean, what is this place?"

"You saw us all and didn't figure it out? Sheesh, I figured you'd be the smart one. The way you sized us all up. We are special. We are different. As María likes to say, we are all budding Bundies. But do not let Alex hear you say that. Alex says we are the children of Uazit, here to fight the war against Order."

As Nettle talked, she placed her fingers against the dark necklace she wore tight against her neck almost absently, as if thinking about something else. The whole sentence was confusing and cryptic, and Jamie did not like that. She knew she needed to understand, but she also knew there would be no straight talk about anything that she wanted to know. The one good thing was that Nettle had momentarily let the façade down and was looking at her with a face that matched her eyes. Jamie wondered if the girl knew she had dropped the flighty air about her, or was no longer lounging so much like a sex kitten but instead sat rigid, like a warrior awaiting the order to pounce. If Nettle was aware, it was a smooth transition made to look unintentional. Perhaps a new type of vulnerability to lure in her prey. Nettle seemed almost serene now. She turned from Jamie and just stared at the wall above the bed and at the painting that hung there. She glanced around at the room she had shown Jamie and then back at the painting. The room that she had told Jamie was Jamie's. That was a thought. It created a moment of silence that Jamie realized they both were sharing as they stared at the painting.

It was a large room with what looked to be a king-sized bed, a few chairs and a couch, a desk with a laptop on it and a swivel chair, and three doors. The furniture, bedding, and walls were all monochrome with solid whites and blacks contrasting with each other in a beautifully stylish way. One entire wall was a large window looking out onto treetops and sky. The kind of view that if she had been alone, Jamie could have stared at for days and never tired of. On the walls, there were black-and-white stills of Chicago throughout its history. Her city's story in frozen life on her walls for her to oversee. And of course, the painting over the bed.

The room was stylishly matching, yet un-obnoxious in its uniformity. It was bare of clutter and knick-knacks beyond a few accent pieces. It was all too clean, yet it looked ready to live in. Everything in the room matched and yet it was not all the same— more like a mix of happy accidents than planned purchases. But like everything here, Jamie did not take it at face value. She had already had trouble with face value. Alex had kicked her need for skepticism up a few notches.

A lot of work had gone into this room. The build, the design, the objects within, the way it had all been set up. A lot of work. Work that had been done for her. Done in a way that looked randomly thrown together, yet every piece here had been picked for her. She was not sure how she knew, but she knew. Someone had looked at her life and studied her enough that they could build a living space that fit her like a glove. A place she could love.

She had thought Alex would just walk away if she had said no, back home. But this room made her wonder. She was special.

Somehow, to this group, she was special. And she did not think they would have let her go so easily, with a simple refusal. It made her wonder what Alex had said to María's parents to get them to say yes. What had happened to Russ' parents to put him on the streets? What had happened with Joe to get him primed for saving? She knew the trap Alex had set for Nettle, but the rest... The rest, she wondered about. What had Alex done? How far would he go if necessary? This room had all been done before Alex had ever met her. He had known she was coming with him, no matter what. This was proof of that. Nobody put in this kind of work on a maybe.

Jamie had to take a breath. A momentary feeling of claustrophobia took hold, and she had to let it go. They had her. She had been collected like some specimen stolen from its home and put on display in a cage. Soon to be taught tricks for her new owner. How could this be? How could she have allowed it? She needed to breathe, to figure out how to be free. She needed it right now. She looked to the doors in her room. Count them. One, two, three. Every door exited from the room, if not the building. See them. One, two three. Ways out. If she needed out, she would get out. The doors were there. She needed to know she could walk through them. One door led out to the hallway they had entered from. It was a quick and obvious method of escape. They'd expect it. She'd never use it unless she wanted to fight. Which was an option she strongly considered. But not if she wanted escape. They were better fighters than she was right now. And there was something about them. Something that made them all seem dangerous in a way that she was only used to being herself.

Another door led into a walk-in closet already stocked with red-and-black clothing in several styles, including what she had seen the others wearing earlier. Nettle assured her they were all tailor-fit to Jamie. More proof that this situation was made for her. How they had gotten her sizes, she shuddered to think. The closet was large and walk-in. There was a vanity on one side of it and a host of drawers and shelves and hangers. The size of it was boggling to Jamie, and honestly, there was a lot of furniture in the closet she had no idea how to use. More importantly, the closet had a window. Small but open to the world. A better option than the obvious front door. She was several floors up, but escape could be possible. She would need to work on the how's. She would need to check the window in her bedroom, in case it was too big to open. Breathe. Take it in; take in how to get out.

The third door led into a fully stocked bathroom with a large claw foot tub, walk-in shower, fancy toilet, and pedestal sink. The whole bathroom was out of a dream. The ceramic of the fixtures was polished and gleaming white—so bright it hurt the eyes when the lights were on, and almost seemed to glow in the darkness when the lights were off. The tiles that covered the walls and floor were a black so dark that they seemed to pull in the light. They sparkled brightly, though in a way that only glazed black tiles can. The towels were all ivory and thick and the first towels in Jamie's life that were almost as long as she was tall. She could barely stand to be in the bathroom without closing her eyes. It was so beautiful and bright and all hers. She did not really want to escape. Not yet. She would give it time, see what happened.

Her entire room was amazing. She had never had her own room before. Never had her own space, and now she had this amazing luxury. It was difficult to understand, to accept. But Nettle gleefully assured her it was true; it was all hers. Above her bed was a painting. A canvas, a dimmed-down canvas with white splotches that stood out against the black walls of her room. The canvas had only a single brushstroke in the middle, that crossed the whole painting like a gash. The stroke was crimson, and it was the only real color in the room that Jamie could see. Because of it, her eyes kept finding the painting. All that color trapped in a single line. It was simple, elegant, and powerful. That one stroke made with a firm and passionate hand. Blood on a bed of snow surrounded by night. It was special. And Jamie understood that she was special, if not yet how. And she understood she needed more information if she wanted to keep her new possessions and sleep under that crimson mark.

"What's with the necklaces you all wear?"

If Nettle had minded the silence or the sudden change in direction of the conversation, she did not reveal it. She laughed her sprinkling laugh. "Oh." Again, with the touch to her throat. "Yes, we all wear them. They are what make us... Well, more us. You will get one as well. Uazit's gifts. Each are made special just for us. She is amazing. She is so individual. Mine is obsidian, beautiful dark obsidian. Don't you just love it? It helps me. It is me. You will learn. It is my power. For now, just know Joe's is ivory, María's is solid gold, and Russ' is turquoise. We are all curious what yours will be, what it will do. Even Hempel is curious, even if she would never admit it."

"Do? What do you mean, do?"

"You will see. They are beautiful, the power they give us. The freedom."

"Who are Uazit and Hempel?"

"Oh, Hempel. She is the other teacher. She is different from us. A different group. But everyone here likes her. And best of all, she is the one bitch Alex don't mess with. He is all yes-ma'am-no-ma'am to her. Even Uazit he argues with, and every other person, he either flirts with, plays, or ignores. But not Hempel. She has a... presence for him, for all of us." Nettle sounded awed as she spoke of the woman. And Jamie wondered at a woman who could cause someone like Nettle to feel like that.

"Alex... Well, we do not know much about Alex, other than he is one BAMF. The show I am sure you got on the way here is what we all get. He is never the same style—not in clothing, not in anything. He just is. The one thing you can rely on is that he will teach you everything. He knows, like, everything. And when we go out, he is our voice of reason. The things he can do! He is amazing. He ain't interested in us, though. Not like that. Not us, not the boys. He is all about teaching with us. No flirting, no arguing. Just teaching. It's frustrating, but he is a great teacher.

"I do know he is older than shit. But, really, he looks mid-twenties, maybe thirty. But that is as much a deception as his clothing. Russ said he heard him and Hempel talking about World War Two once. Like they were both there fighting, so you know that means old. How they can both be so old and look so young, who knows. I mean, he smokes and drinks like crazy. Hopefully, we all have it. Maybe it is one of Uazit's gifts." Nettle again touched her necklace and stared at the painting above the bed. She seemed as mesmerized by it as Jamie. Another kinship they shared.

"Uazit? Who is that?"

"Uazit... Well, Uazit, you need to experience. Not that any of us really do. Well, except Alex. She is... I don't know how to say it. But you will get it." They looked at each other in silence for a moment before Nettle broke the silence with a whisper. "She likes tricks, or something. Hempel calls her the Spider. But you will see. She is beautiful, no worries. Just, you know... Be careful."

The moment was broken by the wiry form of Joe as he came barging through the door and threw himself down next to Nettle. "Why are you keeping her in here? We are all so curious." His whining tone seemed to permeate the boy's entire aura. It filled in everything about him and then oozed off, spilling into the room. Nettle had fallen back into her languidly pouty sex kitten act before Jamie had even realized Joe was coming in.

"Why are you on my bed, kid?" Jamie was irritated. She needed the conversation that had been about to happen, and not the mask firmly back on Nettle's face. She couldn't really complain about the show the girl put on. But some things were more important, and learning what she needed to know was one of them.

At the same time, Jamie's mouth went dry as she looked at the woman on her bed, framed in all her glory and still wearing her workout clothing. Long, bare legs wrapped in tight spandex short shorts and ending in new-looking runners on delicate feet. The tighter top did nothing to hide her curvy figure and athletic frame. Everything about her seemed designed to highlight what Jamie could not help but look at. As Jamie's eyes moved up, she met Nettle's knowing smile. The girl simpered and subtly turned to better highlight the parts previously not seen. Jamie could not but be irritated with Joe for interrupting what else might have been exchanged.

Joe smiled. "Possessive already. I like it. Girlfriend, don't you worry. I have no interest in getting in your bed. Just want to hear what's going on. You know, meet the new competition."

"Joe, what do you need to know? She is from Chicago. Did some B and E. Now, she is here. Same as us all. We were there; now we are here."

Jamie stiffened. She had not mentioned any of her troubles to Nettle, which meant Nettle had been told about Jamie. Had they all been told about her? How deep an act was it? What did they all know but pretend not to know? She was irritated that she had not considered this before. And yet she felt a little protective of her reputation. "Well, I may have done more than break and enter here and there. I broke a few bones as well, when people were irritating." That was simple. Better to be an intimidating brawler than a sneaky old thief when one was trying to exert influence.

And it worked. Joe looked excited, like a newly petted puppy. If he had a tail, it would already be wagging. "You hurt them?"

"If they needed it. Chicago is a tough city. Sometimes you gotta hurt people."

"That is so awesome. We only get to hurt people here if Alex tells us to do it."

Nettle jumped in. "Oh, Joe, keep that mouth hushed. Hurting people is a last resort. We are here to train, to learn how to enjoy our lives. Now, Jamie, you really must shower and get ready for dinner." Everything about what Nettle said and her tone screamed concerned older sister, but it went only so deep. As deep as Joe's whining or his excitement. As deep as Jamie's smile. Jamie saw it all as the façade it was. They all played their parts: the new girl trying to act tough, the kid excited by the shiny and new, and the matron trying to herd them all into safety. They all played their parts, but the game was just a game. She needed to learn the rules if she wanted to be able to really play.

******

"Dominance. The highest goal is dominance," Alex had droned on this morning as they practiced a series of physical exercises. Jamie was already sore, and they were only on the warm-up. Alex continued to lecture, but she barely heard him. She lifted her arms like the others and readjusted last night in her mind.

She had loved the shower the night before, and could not wait to try the claw foot tub. A long, hot shower in her new room followed by using one of the thick, warm towels in her own bathroom. She had tried on one of the pre-made outfits in her closet, and it had fit like a glove. A black-and-red sweater and pant combination with slip-on boat shoes, all over underwear she had found in a drawer. She was amazed by both the fabric and fit of everything. It was all hers, made just for her.

Dinner had been semi-formal in setting, if not clothing, with multiple courses on fancy plates served to each of them and everyone talking at once. Nettle wore a short black skirt and red tube top. Both boys wore black slacks and red collared shirts. María wore the same black skirt as Nettle, but her top was like the black-and-red sweater that Jamie wore. It was weird to see the non-uniform uniform they all had. The combinations were all different, but they obviously had a connected and similar wardrobe to choose from. The color scheme of it all seemed to come from a single source. It made the room match, but in a way that felt individual. A disorderly puzzle that fit together in harmony even as it clashed.

Conversation was light and entertaining. Everyone there seemed quite good at talking about nothing and still having a fun time. They felt connected without really making a connection. Jamie was asked many questions. The others were hungry for information about her, even as their eyes seemed to judge everything but her words. Those clawing, claiming eyes that searched her every look to parse it down and study it like a bug on a pin. It was a more glorious evening than Jamie had ever had. She felt like she had spent the night dancing with a great partner. After it all, she had climbed into her own big bed and slept like a baby. Only to be awakened to this—calisthenics and lectures.

It seemed that Alex came from a time before classrooms had desks. Jamie was informed that they would spend their days listening to him while they followed a strenuous workout regime that he had devised. Joe had informed her that even the "light" classes, where they were expected to respond at length and ask questions, were done while running, moving, doing yoga, or lifting. The only physical exercise Alex did not teach was how to fight. That was left to Hempel. Alex wanted to ensure that their blood was pumping and their minds were alert all at once. Speaking while working out had the added benefit María had mentioned—that people tended to give concise answers when trying to breathe. How well it was working Jamie could not tell. Her side hurt and her lungs burned, and the barking of the lecture seemed far away in relation to her legs growing heavier and her arms wanting to shake. Not to mention the fact that she had just missed the day's first lecture as she thought about the night before. The lessons had moved past daily recitation, and she had barely heard.

"Socrates was considered the wisest man who ever lived, by the Oracle, because he knew he knew nothing. Now, if that is all that Socrates knew, how is it that some of the Dialogues are filled with him teaching what he knew?" Even without being able to look up, Jamie could feel the stern eyes of her teacher upon her. His voice was even, his words almost kind. But she felt the cold, unforgiving metal under the words, intertwined with the voice. They would learn his lessons, that tone said. They would learn his physical forms, that tone whispered. He would accept no other outcome; that was what went unspoken and screamed with every quiet word. "Joseph, stop breathing like a dying pig on the sands of a Pacific island, and answer my question." Joe was barely breathing hard, and Jamie hated him for it. She was struggling to keep up.

But she had to smile as Joe tried to answer and was obviously working harder to both breathe and talk. His answers came short and clipped, as a result. "The Dialogues are only Plato. No Socrates there. Socrates is gone."

"Explain Joseph's answer, Maríalin."

To Jamie's horror, María seemed barely to have broken a sweat. She merely moved through the motions like they were strolling through a light breeze she was enjoying. Her voice came out in a smooth, even tempo. "The Dialogues are written by Plato. Socrates wrote nothing. Socrates, as he was, is not in the Dialogues, but only a student's claimed perception of him. We know his thoughts only through what others wrote. We are, therefore, unsure of what he really thought and have no way of being sure."

"Correct, and trust me, Plato's characterizations of people were not always accurate. To this, I can attest. It is believed that the early Dialogues can be trusted, but the later ones are often considered Plato's own theories, parroted by his master. Regardless, we must be suspicious of them all and of the writings of others, as they are hearsay, interpretations of what was heard. That stated, let us move forward as if the earlier Dialogues are representative. Russel, what do we think Socrates wanted to teach?"

Russ looked pained to be called upon, but when he spoke, it was with conviction. Barely a hitch in his throat to reveal how hard he was pushing in the workout. "How to question."

"Correct. Socrates questioned everything. When faced with Euthyphro, he questioned the very ability of persons to know what is right or wrong. The story of Euthyphro is simple. Euthyphro's father had grown upset at a worker for killing a slave. The father had the worker bound and thrown in a ditch. He liked his slaves, and they were his to kill, not this other man's. Especially not a man who did not even own land. The worker died in the ditch, because he was forgotten about. Often, this is the case when you throw a person in a ditch—that they become forgettable. Well, the worker died, and the father was taken up on charges. Euthyphro, as the prosecutor, took the case on himself. Socrates, coming upon Euthyphro, rejoiced, for a man to take such a position against his own father must truly have known what was just and what was unjust. A man like this could teach Socrates piety. So they talked, and Socrates pissed him off with all this talk of ethics. They did not discuss the blaring, obvious ethical question of how shitty it is to be anyone who does not own land and is therefore disposable. Instead, they discussed the relationship between a lawyer and his dad. Socrates asked what made what Euthyphro did just.

"Euthyphro first claimed that what he was doing by prosecuting a murder was just, even if it was his dad. People should prosecute murders. Socrates' questions made clear that Euthyphro's actions were merely a potential specific example, but prosecuting one's own father wasn't, in itself, an universal example of justice.

"Second, Euthyphro claimed that his prosecution of his father was good because it was pleasing to the gods. Gods like murders to get prosecuted, I suppose. But Socrates asked if the gods were fickle and justice was merely their opinion. Does that not make justice just an opinion? I mean, if God can change her mind on what is right or wrong, then right or wrong can change. There are many gods; if they disagree, how does one test justice? A definition of justice that relies on gods simply does not work.

"Euthyphro amended his answer in his third attempt, saying that all the gods had to love something for it to be just. Socrates asked an interesting question, hitting at a crux that is important even in modern mythological systems. Is a thing just because God loves it, or does God love it because it is just? Nettle, explain why this is important."

"It determines if the attribute exists before or because the outside influence decides it has the attribute. It reveals if it can be changed like an opinion. It also determines if the outside decider could potentially be wrong. What is independent of what?"

"Correct, mostly. Socrates was attempting to show Euthyphro that his argument was pointless. It is like asking why a steak is delicious and saying it is delicious because the dog likes to eat it. But it is understandable. The steak was delicious well before the dog tried it—that is, if a word like 'delicious' is to have any real value beyond preference. If a word's meaning is based on preference, then it cannot be a fact. Truths and facts are only truths for Socrates if we can prove them. Wanting or believing them has no impact on their truth value. Preferences cannot be truths. Socrates and Euthyphro engaged in five main arguments that you will need to read tonight. But it is important to understand what Plato is showing us here. He was not showing us Socrates' answer; he was showing us his master's question. Socrates was asking for a rule, a statement. A statement he never gives; he just asks. There are goddesses we can all serve, but we have a deeper duty. How do we decide that duty? Jasmine, what is 'goodness' in this theory of Socrates?"

Jamie was out of breath. It took her a moment to realize that Alex had used her full name. She could feel her lungs burn from the movements, and see how jerky her attempt to move from form to form was, compared to everyone else's. She thought about everything that had been said. She looked at the puzzle, thought it through. She took a deep, striving breath and tried to answer without stopping—a thing even harder than she had imagined. "Socrates was so smart, and he couldn't figure it out—means it's likely not answerable."

Alex looked at her in silence for several minutes. Minutes that worried Jamie. What was the price of failure, of getting it wrong? She kept up with the movements, outwardly calm.

"Your answer is erroneous and not really valid, yet it holds a kernel of truth. First, just because someone else cannot find an answer is not indicative that there is no answer. A failure to swim to shore is not the same as there being no shore. Even if there is no proof of an answer, that is not indicative that there is no answer. 'The absence of proof is not the proof of absence.' All of that said, all good things can be perceived as negatives, and all negative things can be justified as goodness in specific circumstances. It is widely believed that Socrates was searching for an answer, that he believed there could be an answer. But this fails to be proven.

"First, Socrates may have thought the attribute of being good was merely made-up thoughts with no real answer to what it is at the heart of goodness. That the very idea of 'justice' is silly and nonsense. It is possible that his line of questioning of

Euthyphro and others was an attempt to reveal this disbelief in imaginary gods and rules we call good and bad. Regardless of what we believe about these topics, it is unlikely Socrates believed in this kind of relativism. It is, from other readings and this one, likely that Socrates, instead, believed there was something to be said about the attribute known as goodness, or justice. Look specifically at the conversation before he died in your readings. But it is equally likely that he did not believe there was a method to know goodness or justice. Socrates created a question that seems impossible to answer. It seems obvious that, like a koan, it is meant not to be answered, but only considered until enlightenment comes. It is unlikely that Socrates took the extra step from 'we cannot know,' to 'there is nothing there.' He would have known that a thing being unprovable does not disprove it.

"That said, a thing we can prove nothing about is useless to us, beyond being an example. We cannot know what is good or just, and we cannot prove what makes a thing fit the mold. So we will ignore them as actual, real concepts. We will, instead, in the next lesson, look to societal demands on us and how we can fit within them. There will be no assumption of good or evil, only what is beneficial to us and what is detrimental to us. You will understand more as we delve in. For now, understand that it is wisdom we desire. Wisdom is the one good that we will seek here. It is the only good that we will not divest ourselves of. Each of you will hold it as your candle that will guide you. You will experience the world in any way that allows for more experience, and thus more wisdom, to grow. This is your duty to freely experience the world. I will guide you until you no longer need a guide."

Jamie faltered. That did not feel right. It was not what she had been taught. She could not help it; her mouth asked before her mind considered. "What about murder? Isn't it always bad?"

Alex paused to look at her. Again, with his silence. He weighed her this time. Not her answer. Not the words. Her. His eyes weighed her. "We can all think of a good reason to kill someone." It was all he said. His only response given with the cold eyes she had come to expect. He seemed to be stating a fact they all agreed to.

MEMORIES OF THE NEW REALITY

Jamie touched the ruby collar at her throat. She could feel the power entering her through it. The power screamed raw and pure. It screamed everything she wanted. The collar screamed power. The pain of the power filled her with an animal joy. She raised her hand before her to see the sparks as she let the power burn through her. The power hurt, but she was learning to shape it. Learning what she could do. She could breathe in the piney air of the forest around her. The power filled her, the calm settled into her, and she could reflect on how she had gotten here.

Her short time at the school had been life-changing. The daily workouts and lessons continued and would continue. They ran regularly across the mountain terrain and swam in the river behind the house. They practiced all nature of physical movement, from dance to martial arts. They learned about the world in new and exciting ways. They just kept learning, moving, becoming. Every minute of her time here, Jamie learned more and more.

She learned how to manage danger. The landscape was green and wild and sharp. Everything, from the rocks that pushed up from the earth to the needles on the trees, she found were sharp. The animals were all potentially dangerous, and the weather itself could kill her. She learned, though. She learned that danger can be found anywhere, anytime, and yet a healthy dose of respect often kept you safe. She learned to run through trees and over mountain saddles like the wind. As she became faster and got in better shape, she learned to love those runs. They gave her a chance to become wild and free, like everything around her.

She learned that the dangers were not just in the natural world. The other four students and two teachers were just as dangerous. Jamie had been struck to the ground in practice and had exchanged barbs in conversation. They were animals being trained though unable to be tamed. Jamie was taught over and over that the world was dangerous and that she could overcome it.

She learned the other kids. There were only the five of them. Each so different and yet that running thread of sameness that ran underneath the surface. Nettle had said that Uazit was a collector of diversity and here it showed. Not just in race or socioeconomic background but in personality. They were like a conglomeration of different personalities. A microcosm of the world and all the people in it. How they were all framing into a group, Jamie was not sure. Maybe the part of them under the mask was similarly empty enough that they could mesh. Jamie knew that the masks were all she really saw of her classmates, except on the rare occasions people dropped them.

Joe often tagged around behind the others. He was the consummate little brother, constantly asking questions and trying to be part of the pack while learning everything about everyone. He claimed a level of spirituality, even in the face of disbelief by the rest of the group. He was one of those kids who was a nuisance—one you humored because he was just so puppy-like. Jamie found herself becoming protective of him, especially in light of Russ' bad influence on his behavior. Joe seemed sad at times, but his sadness was always quickly covered with a happy smile and a quick recovery. He preferred his clothing looser than any of the rest did, and he wore it with a style of relaxed energy.

María was the princess who filled a room with her smile and manners. Jamie had yet to see her say a single inappropriate thing, as if such uncouth words were beneath her. Well, mostly. There was the moment when Russ had slapped her on the ass and she had thrown him to the ground in an arm-wrenching maneuver that Jamie honestly was surprised did not break his arm. María had demanded in that moment, holding his arm close to breaking, that he accept his mistake and promise not to do it again. He had tried to resist, but one look into María's eyes and he had relented. Jamie was unsure why María had not broken his arm. There was violence buried in the princess, a violence that ran deep and pure in a way that Jamie envied. But that was underneath. On the surface was the prim princess who never looked haggard, only regal. Thick red lips that commanded a room. Her clothing always had the feel of formal attire, even when she wore the same shorts and tank everyone else wore during the workouts. She often added a small touch of personalization to each outfit. A brooch here or a piece of jewelry there.

Russ—well, Russ was a perv and a joker. He often responded to questions or situations with humor that at first seemed like silly and offensive innuendo, but after some thought seemed passive-aggressive, and after more thought seemed brutally honest. Jamie thought the wit needed to pull it off revealed a mind inside, but if so, it was a mind he rarely shared with the group, besides through his barbs. He constantly attempted to flirt with the girls while concentrating most of his fire on María. Jamie assumed that the ice princess act was a challenge to him. Few things he said were not innuendo, and nothing he said was not filtered through a smile. In the end, it was apparent that he went to great lengths to get a reaction. It was also apparent that he rarely planned what the reaction would be or how it would affect him personally. He just seemed to enjoy causing the ripple. María had said that she considered him a child who liked to see the fireworks go off, no matter how close he happened to be standing. His attire showed off an obvious obsession with lifting that accentuated his broad shoulders. The tight fit of his clothing choices rivaled only Nettle's in their obvious attempt to attract the eye. They seemed in competition to see who could show the most skin with tighter and tighter clothing.

Lastly—or firstly, as it were, there was Nettle. Nettle was Nettle. Being around her must have been what it was like to be on set with Marilyn Monroe, minus the drugs and depression. In a group of people who would always be at the center of any room, she was at the center of their room. Nettle exuded nymphet and alpha overachiever all at once. She always knew the answer to questions and never looked out of place. She was the closest in personality to Alex, in Jamie's mind, mostly because she could change her nymphet mask for a variety of others that fit the occasion. She often took on a matronly role with the other teens and worked to guide them, much like a sheep dog with unruly goats. For all her flighty giggles on the surface, she was the dominant one in the group, and the others obeyed her without question. Her clothing was always stylishly created out of very little pieces of tight fabric. Jamie was in awe of Nettle's greatness. The students all held her in the highest respect. The two teachers used her to help, partly because she had been here so long and partly because of her obvious ability. She was, in all things, a force of nature, and even Alex at times stepped out of her way.

Jamie was learning that they were a team. The practice they did and education they received were often geared toward how they needed to work together. Their training was shaping them into a pack that could move through complex patterns as a unit while still making individual choices. Jamie could, by the end of the first week, move through a complex pattern while being directed by a teammate with almost no verbalized instructions. It was an intense grouping for a team that found it almost impossible to make external connections.

The other teacher she had met when she began to learn martial arts and weapons. Alex, it seemed, taught the non-fighting forms while lecturing, and Hempel taught the violence. To Alex, she was Hempel, and every word he spoke to her was filled with respect. Everyone else here had long hair, but Hempel's was closely cropped and tightly curled. It was black as night and hugged her face in a way that seemed to frame her caramel features. She was Native Alaskan—said to have been born on the ice and left to die. She had raised herself there, learning from birth to survive. She had a sharp beauty that was almost as piercing as the hazelnut eyes she stared out from.

She was beautiful in the same way that a blizzard was beautiful. Snow falling and covering the earth. A winter's night is beautiful in a way nothing else is. Beautiful in an unequaled way. Such a clear, pure blanket over the world, hiding away all the life underneath, giving it a chance to die and be reborn. A thick protective shield so that next year, life can have a new world. It keeps on falling in thick, fluffy flakes of soft coldness. It is interesting that so many people think of cold as hard and unyielding, as if the only thing cold they have ever had to deal with is the ice in their fridge. Yet the snowy flakes falling on a winter night are soft and light. A gentle touch of frozen grace. The freezing wind, likewise, is not hard and emotionless, but fierce and sharp in embracing those who face it. It can pass through any defense through its complete yielding to all things. The cold is so much more than hard and frozen. It is a multitude of beauties contained in a single embrace of feeling. The cold is a beautiful moment filled with beautiful moments. Standing next to Hempel was like standing in that blizzard, a calm-filled storm that never stopped moving while filling the world with serene stillness.

Hempel dressed as a consummate professional, in matronly clothing that covered her obviously athletic frame. Her clothing was often homespun wool, with decorative patterns around the collars and cuffs. She was the only one here who had no necklace fit tightly around her neck. She wore no jewelry, unless you counted the two half-moon blades that hung at her belt. She had the only smile in the entire group that felt genuine, but that might have been because she usually kept a serious look on her face. She had what Jamie's brother had called "resting bitch face." Ironically, though, here it made her seem more mothering and loving. A deep birthmark spread along one side of her face and dipped down her neck, under her collar. It was not marring, though; it added to her beauty. It was dappling on the hide of a mustang. It was part and parcel of what made her the most stunning woman Jamie had ever seen.

Hempel spoke little and saw much. Jamie had learned to expect single-word responses to her many questions—often the most literal answers. Those short, accurate answers cut through what more words would have wasted time getting wrong. It was beginning to feel like the woman never made basic assumptions, even blaringly obvious ones. She simplified the world into easy-to-manage parts and then crushed each part to dust.

Jamie had, in her short time, only heard Hempel give one

long speech, and it was in answer to a question. They had been finishing up a sparring match when Joe had asked, "Why do we do this? Why are we learning to fight?"

"You prepare to fight the war."

"But why do we need to fight a war?"

Hempel stood quietly for a minute, looking at Joe. Her piercing hazel eyes seemed to devour him. Then she spoke. "As you know, I am not of Uazit. I am Chosen by the great Tala, Raven. Each Trickster differs in how and why they approach this fight. But one thing we do have in common. To see this thing, look at your master. Look at Alex. He is different from other people. He is free of fear. There is another thing that chains him, but fear and worry are anathema to his existence. What a child he remains! Older than all of us, and yet, here he is, free of the one prison everyone eventually finds time to build.

"Look at love. In youth, the screams of adoration come so easily. As we grow older, the flaming/burning ability of youth to speak honestly leaves us. It hides away behind walls. Not the feeling of love, but the expression of it. The words used by children are filled with a parade of colors that adults dare not admit to seeing. There are no humans seen after a certain age— only fortresses built from perceived experiences. They hide away in those monuments to safety. Hide away within themselves, survivors of a lifelong war called other people. This is the question—how to get them free from these mental prisons that they built to protect themselves.

"That is the gift we wish to give the world and Order wishes to suppress. That is what my family died for. That is the war you will fight. That is why you are Chosen. It is up to you to decide what that purity of freedom is worth."

The team had quietly digested her words. The silence filled the room, filled them. It devoured Jamie where she stood and filled her with righteousness.

Hempel seemed so much nicer than Alex, and yet Joe was correct. The forms she had them work through were meant to prepare them for violence and little else. She seemed an expert in weapon after weapon, while also working them through a multitude of styles of unarmed combat. Her every move was that of a dancer. There was a sadness in her, though, an echo of loss.

Alex had grown on Jamie. He was often quiet and professional. He tended to be short and direct in how he spoke, but at odd moments, he would begin to talk and just monologued for hours about the smallest things. Usually things he enjoyed. Often food or drink. Once about tobacco. Jamie had learned from him more about coffee than she had ever wanted to know. He seemed to take pride in all of the things he did. The smallest act required the greatest concentration. He never spoke of where he was from or what he had done before taking on the tutoring of very special teens.

His accent changed with conversations, as did the colloquialisms he dropped in day-to-day language. Jamie had heard him speak a variety of languages. His clothing changed in style and substance at almost every turn. She had seen him change clothing six times in a single day for no reason she could tell, other than whim. The one unifying feature seemed to be the quality of the clothing he chose. Even those outfits that looked untidy had the underlying look of hand-stitching, if anyone bothered to look. He seemed to be an ever-changing character actor who just could not settle on who to be.

He was a good teacher. His lessons were like no education Jamie had ever been part of before. He worked them through a multitude of never-ending, always-changing calisthenics accompanied by lessons about over a million different topics. He seemed to love to run, especially through the deep wilds of the land around them.

Jamie learned about history and, through it, science and philosophy. Alex taught that nothing interdepended on anything else. His lessons felt more like stories. He showed them the world through the lives of those who had lived in it. There were no long talks of complex ideas. There were people living their lives and shaping their world. If they learned about a woman in the 1970s, they learned her thoughts and actions and the events around her. They learned about her life and through her, the science she revolutionized and the world she changed. Alex spoke often as if he had known these people and lived through their lives. He was an engaging teacher who seemed more like a storyteller.

He really dug in, though, when the lessons turned to how to act around other people. He would talk about interpersonal communications and how to work a crowd. The best way to pull a wallet from a jacket pocket, and the passwords people most liked. The many words and phrases that would cause certain reactions and how best to funnel those reactions into useful outcomes. He taught the variable of people in the world and how to direct the traffic of their lives.

In the end, he was teaching them mostly how to think and very little about what to think. The many ways to study what is. It was a crash course in working their way through life. Jamie never stopped moving mentally or physically. She could feel herself changing.

But Alex's lessons were secondary, though. They had become shadowed in her mind. They were daily attempts to pass the time and build her up. But she did not really need the lessons; she just enjoyed them. They were making her better, but not in a way that mattered. She had understood this from the moment Alex had walked into her room and dropped the deeply crimson-colored ruby necklace onto the bed and walked back out. There seemed to be no connectors between the large gems that had a muted glow in the dark room, and yet, they held together to form a beautifully wrought full throat piece that looked almost like a collar. There were dark red hooks on the ends to connect it into a fully formed circle once it was on.

Alex had not told her to put it on or what it was. He had moved silently and slowly, as he almost always did. Walked in and dropped it like an old coin and then was gone. The necklace was in no special box or bag, and there seemed to be no real ceremony to the delivery. He did not seem to even care if Jamie noticed him. But he did meet her gaze.

He looked at her as he stopped, gazing down on her lying on her bed. Her breath had caught in anticipation of what he may want here in her room, with her in bed and him standing above her. She had not yet seen the necklace in his hand, and Alex was an attractive man, if a bit older than she usually liked, and sadly male. Not to mention that he was her teacher and the team's mentor. But her mind could not help but wander to his strong arms and deep chest as he stood above her bed, looking at her with his intense blue eyes. His hair hung down loose, messy, partially over his face. His lips slightly pursed as if he had something to say, but no words would come. He was in all things an unstoppable force of nature, and Jamie could not help but wonder how that would translate here with her. Her stomach tightened and her mind spun.

If Alex saw her desire in her eyes or guessed her thoughts, he gave no indication. He made no sounds. His face was a closed mask—looking at her the way a woman looks at a wall—and a boring wall, at that. There was neither a grand dramatic gesture, nor violently satisfying ravishment to come. There was not even a "here ya go." Alex merely dropped the necklace and turned and walked back out. Not a single word, not a single signal that he had even seen her. At first, Jamie was disappointed, but then her fingers touched the first ruby.

It was cold and warm all at once, under her fingers. It caught the light from her lamps and seemed to suck it in, filling each gem with an inner glow that breathed back out as a cold light. She marveled at the beauty in her grasp. It was the most marvelous piece of jewelry she had ever seen. She could not help but pick it up and gaze into it.

That was the moment her real study had begun. The

moment she found herself. The second she snapped the ruby collar around her neck, she felt it—the power and the goddess that was focusing the power through her. Power overtook her and drove her to the ground, as her body began to relearn muscle movements she had never used, and her mind began to open to possibilities that had previously been impossible. She was not sure if she had screamed through the pain, but she knew she had wanted to. She wanted to scream and scream until her voice tore and her mind broke. She wanted to beg Alex to come back to help her. But through it all, what she really wanted was the necklace, the power, and the pain to never end. The memory of wanting to scream ended with the crimson darkness that took her as she slammed into the floor. She could feel her body convulsing, but it was for this single occasion, a stranger's body.

That moment was a moment of awakening for her entire life. Everything that had come before came into focus and stopped making sense. It had all been a dream where she had hidden who she was. But this was her; this was an opening to the creature that hid behind her smile. The feel of power within her drove her and empowered her. The necklace had pulsed with a low burgundy light that shone from the rubies that made it up. As it pulsed, Jamie could feel herself growing, becoming. As Nettle had said it would, the necklace had made her more her. Her life became the pulse. She became who she had always been.

Jamie had always known she was different from other people. She felt little connection to anything about others, and often found that they expected her to feel things that she was just not sure how to feel. She had lived her life in an alien landscape that had embraced her and attempted to make demands of her she barely understood. She had acted on whims few other people she knew would give in to. She often found herself in trouble, due to her inability to explain why she gave in. She felt like a constant fraud, because she knew she was empty inside, matching her face to the face others wanted to see. She had always wanted to show her true self to someone, but she had no idea what her true self might be. She had always known she was a mess of differences and had sought to fix them. But there was no fixing, no need to fix, because now she was herself.

All that self-doubt was over the moment the power took her. She was still different. Still disconnected from others. Still an unemotional being who would never make sense of those around her. Still impulsive and whimsical. Still empty inside and still nothing more than a mimic attempting to manipulate those around her. She was still all those things. But now, the struggle was over. She was ok. What she was... was ok. All the pieces she had always believed were broken were found to be perfect. They had just been misfiled by a lifetime of other people's words. Those words were just words now; she was free of such pathetic chains.

She felt Uazit within her, within the necklace. She felt the acceptance fill her, the deep abiding acceptance that Uazit had for all her children. If Jamie had been capable of true emotion, she would have cried. Instead, she smiled and laughed to finally be seen by someone who could like her, let alone love her. Uazit did not love Jamie the mask; she loved Jamie the nothing.

This was the love letter she had waited her entire life to hear. The full embrace of another that was building something within her. The warm touch of another mind that looked upon her and wanted her. Its light touch slipped along the edges of her being, and she felt the tingle of joy that tickled her core. Her body reacted as her mind gloried in the embrace. The power and love built within her as the necklace pulsed and continued to feed her obsessive need for more power. Jamie had much to learn, but this first lesson she embraced with gusto. It had felt like nothing she had ever felt before in her life. Everything else was secondary. The lessons continued, but they had new purpose.

Alex's lessons took on a new meaning for her. Alex seemed to echo both her new feelings and the whisperings of Uazit in her mind. Over the course of days, he taught them the basics of their new history, the path of war they would be expected to fight.

Sitting there in the mountains, the hard tree bark pushing against her back, Jamie remembered putting on the necklace, and she imagined the history that Alex had taught them. The lesson still fresh in her mind's eye. His words like a projector, filling her mind with images of long ago.

It had been a slow run through the trees and up the mountain trails, the slap-slap of runners as Alex's voice filled the morning air. He had spoken of the war in which they would be soldiers. The tale of how the world had reached a point to need them. His voice had been deep and gravelly that day, telling the ancient tale as fact.

"The war started well before any human living can remember—the war between freedom and control. It has always been fought in secret from the humans. The speaking animals and spirits of the land took sides and embraced one way or the other. The forces of control came out strong, and the forces of freedom came back stronger.

"There were those that wanted to be left alone, but in time, no one could go without a side for protection. Those in the cracks would be ground into dust. And so, the world of spirits was split between ideas about how to rule the world. But it took time to reach the point of ideological difference we see today. The war did not start there, for back then, all divergent attitudes had a place.

"How did the war start? Some said when a baby was born.
Others said there was a monster, the Monster. It killed
whomever and did whatever it wanted. It was ruled by no
kingdom, held back by no borders. No one could stop the
Monster's gleeful rampage of vivacious life. It lived a life of excess
that few others had ever experienced. And it struck fear and envy
in the hearts of all who perceived it.

"But there were those that did not fear the Monster. One
day, in the open seas, the Queen of Order was enraged and so
confronted it. It is said she did not wish to, but then who would?
It was the Monster. It acted in such an uncouth way, she could
not accept it. And so, they fought. And she drove it from the sea,
but she could not kill it. The Queen, fearing what would come
from the altercation, built her army, picked her Champions. But
with it all, she could not find and defeat the Monster. It lived, and
so she built and prepared.

"At the same time, the four Gods dedicated to freedom,
known as Tricksters, had traveled the world. They found
themselves meeting up together to discuss the Monster, but they
became more worried by the growing army of Order. The
Tricksters feared the force would be used to cut back on their
whimsical lifestyle. It is no small discomfort when those that

disagree with you build an army, regardless of its intended use. Spider, Raven, Coyote, and Fox agreed that each would create their Chosen and create weapons to be used. They feared the growing might of Order, and they wished to be ready to face it. The Cold War of the Monster began.

"But it would not last even the length of a single human pregnancy. Spider's Chosen were slaughtered by the Monster in combat. Spider was furious, and violently so. The Monster in all its glory had done her wrong. She chained it and buried it deep within history, succeeding through her sheer maliciousness where the Queen and the Gods had failed. Spider had long been feared for her whimsically malicious nature, and here she proved their fears had been justified.

"But the Queen was unhappy, so she and Spider argued over the Monster. The other Gods came to Spider's defense. Without the Monster to unite them all, the armies of Order were free to do battle with the Chosen of the Gods. The Queen determined that the Gods and their whimsies had become as dangerous as the Monster had been, so she sought to control them.

"The Queen knew that the Tricksters, especially, would never bow to the rule of Order without being forced, so she commanded her armies to remove them. She believed that without them, the other Gods would step in line.

"The armies of Order then attacked. They came at the Tricksters and their freedom strongly. And the Tricksters came back stronger. The cold war had grown hot. But nobody wished the world to die, so they fought in secret, and the Champions of Order fought the Chosen on battlefields hidden from the view of the masses. Humans were left out of it, and only the spirits of the land and talking animals took part.

"The other Tricksters feared Spider's legendary maliciousness, so they begged her not to join the fight. The Monster had killed her Chosen, and they asked her not to create more to replace them. So she merely watched. The War raged with her on the sidelines.

"The war is ancient now, my children. It has spent all its time killing many and tearing apart more. The Chosen fought the many armies of Order. The Monster is shackled, and the Chosen forgot it, the armies forgot it. And now they fight, one for control and one for freedom. They fight now for ideology. It is a war that has raged in secret for generations.

"The war was mostly balanced, until recently. Order came into possession of key Champions tempted from their families. They decimated the warriors of freedom, one by one. Coyote fights a guerilla war against a great black snake upon the land.

Fox has not been seen for years, the fate of her or her Chosen unknown, though in legend they fight from the shadows. Raven's forces were decimated; they killed the Chosen of Raven down to one and took the great Raven Sword. Raven awaits the return of the sword before teaching a new breed. Raven and Coyote knew the war's loss was coming if they did not act. So they approached Spider and begged her to help. She came and picked her Chosen. She picked each of you, and you will win this war." Alex signaled them to stop upon the cliff edge they had reached.

The view spread out before them in broken rocks and climbing trees. An entire world was down there, vast and wild. The team breathed heavily, as Alex had pushed them hard up the mountainside, but Alex himself looked as if he had just rolled out of bed. He gazed out over that broad, breathtaking vista as if he was looking through it, back into a time that had led him here.

"You will win this war. You are Chosen. Special. I will teach you your duty to free the world from all control." And then he was off, running quietly as they all trailed behind him back toward their home. Jamie had listened. She had heard the story and at the same time, felt it. The emotions of each moment of the tale she had felt from her necklace. She had decided then that she needed to learn more, learn to control the necklace and use it to embrace its power. The memory of that run and the feelings it had engendered stayed with her. She knew she would be a warrior, and that she would fight this war for her goddess.

All of that had led to now. It had led to her solitary run into the daylight. The stop by the stream and the sitting by the tree. It had led to her reflection on her time here. It had led to a constant testing and strengthening of her power and her body. Sitting against the tree, filtering her memories. Sitting against the tree, practicing her power.

While all these thoughts and memories passed through her mind, Jamie sat with her back to a dark pine, listening to the river burble and run past her. The sun dappled here and there through the tree cover in ever-shifting patterns created by a mix of sighing, rustling trees and clouds interacting with a moving sun. Birds chirped in the distance, and a chipmunk chattered angrily somewhere above. Jamie could feel the insects in the air and on the ground around her. Flitting here and scurrying there. The clamoring of life all around her.

Every piece of the world around her was connected. It was all one thing, pulsing with being. That being had veins she could see, veins of life that hurt her mind's eye. The life that permeated this area pulsed inward, as her necklace pulsed with its crimson glow. So many things beating like hearts all around her, beating somehow in unison even as the many beats were a disjointed chaos that filled the air with competing sounds. It was raw and painful to let it pulse through her.

Jamie held her hands before her, fingers splayed. She felt the power surge out into her hands; she pushed it, allowed it, stretched it out in the daylight. Her hands tensed into claws as the power sparked into bright zigzagging lines that covered her arms like elbow-length gloves. It hurt—oh, god, it hurt. Uazit shared her power, but raw power hurt. It was a thing to love. Jamie could feel the moment, and she reached out to grab it.

There was a second between seconds that Jamie was capable of holding for just a single second. But that second was enough. When her fingers encircled it, her mind clicked. The chittering of the chipmunk slowed, and the beat of a dragonfly's wings turned from blindingly blurry, to slow, to frozen. The world was frozen. The moving, dappling light remained in its current formations, and the trees stopped their sighing. The world paused; even the river's constant burble was gone.

It was only her. Her breath. Her mind. Her power. She sat in the silent stillness like a Buddha from an ancient tale. The power burned; it arced from her to the world, and the single second she was able to grab held strong against her palm. The exertion of it beat at her, and the pain in her hand began to burn. But she could not help it; she laughed. And with the laugh, her concentration broke and the dragonfly flew away to the sounds of the forest around them. The moment was beautiful, and her laughter filled all the seconds she had not grabbed.

The power still pulsed under her skin; the necklace still drew it in and spread it throughout her. She could feel the presence of Uazit within her. That was not always a constant, the presence, but it was here now, strong. She could hear the Spider Queen's voice like an itching at the back of her mind. She never knew what was said, but it always left her with a feeling of knowing what it meant. Uazit was pleased with her, pleased with her strength. They would free the world together. They would free the world with happy accidents and secret assaults the world would never understand. They would be its saviors.

TRAVEL THE HARD WAY

The morning sun had barely touched the sky as they sat upon the grass in a haphazard mess of organization, all facing Alex who was dancing power along his hands. He did not look up at them, but instead at the green lightning that moved between his fingers and along his palms in a riot of light and beauty.

"The power is raw and wild. Any attempt to tame it will end in painful disaster. It is here, screaming at us in a song that touches upon the very core of our beings. You will never tame it, but you can focus it. If you give in, it can provide many gifts." As he spoke, the power in his hand began to glow brighter and then solidify into a dark green ball he held in his open palm. He then began to juggle, and the ball began to multiply. Jade balls of glass flickered through the air. Alex expanded the ever-widening circle of more and more balls.

"The power can provide the links you need to the

moments you wish to hold on to." And the world began to slow and stop, until the sun stood high in the air, unmoving. The chirp of the birds had been cut mid-chirp, and the wind that had been a gentle breeze a moment before was stilled. The balls of jade that had been spinning through the air only moments before were frozen in space, a giant circle between Alex and the team. It was a moment in time, what Jamie called the second between seconds. But somehow, Alex had not only brought himself to this serenity, he had also brought his students with him. They could share the moment he grasped and held.

"The power has no limits other than your own self-restrictions." The balls began to spin, and in a flash of light that burned the retinas, they were thrown outward around the team, forming a perfect spinning circle of light that they all sat within. The balls glowed now with their inner light and filled the clearing with a green glow that bleached out the sun. The glow created a feeling for Jamie of looking at the world through jade lenses, and her awe at the spectacle meant it took a minute for her to realize that the sounds of nature and life had returned. Time was moving forward again.

"You are the Chosen of the Mother of all Tricksters. She has gifted you her presence, and you can tap into that to move mountains and drain seas. With the right focus, you can accomplish anything. The power comes with pain. It is an electric current you let pass through your body to light the world around you. A live wire you must grasp. That is not a thing you can expect to do without pain. That is not a thing you can expect to do without addiction." As Alex spoke, the balls slowly began to spin, and the power within his hands grew into flames, flames that took on shapes. Shapes that mixed and matched the words Alex spoke, illustrating the story his words only labeled.

"The power, in all the ways it fills you, will be the greatest pleasure you will ever know. It will drive you to use it, to hold it, to reach for it. You will exist in a reality where that pain and that pleasure will be intertwined. Where joy and sorrow will never again be separate. You will see the rose. You will see its petals filled with beauty at the same time as you see the thorns that hide beneath them. You will understand that the rose lives and will die. There will never be the fragrance of life without the scent of death clinging to it. You will know the seeds of birth growing in the ashes as the world burns.

"This power will be your lifelong temptation. You will know freedom through succumbing to that temptation. Let us begin to embrace our power. Please begin."

The students held up their hands, and the clearing became a mass of colors and light as each hand became encircled, first in the lightning, and then in the flame of their own particular color. As Russ raised his hands, a turquoise flame jetted up into the morning sky, pushing the green light of Alex's power away from Russ' hands and arms. His face was awash with blue, then green, then blue, then green as each flame in his hand flickered and danced. María held a ball of gold in her hand, and the light of it bathed her in its golden light. The serenity of her smile was echoed in the beauty of her light.

Looking at Joe was like staring at a light bulb. The white light that shone in his hand was too bright to see what he had created, and even as it toned down into an ivory bar, the light defied a direct look. Nettle held before her an obsidian sword. The darkness of her light made no attempt to outshine the jade of Alex's power that pulsed around her. Instead, it seemed to intertwine itself with the other light, creating veins of black that spread out like roots, changing the tints and shades of the jade until the air around her looked less like a glowing green and more like a painting of subtle beauty and change.

Jamie was not sure what she could create with her power. She knew the others had been practicing longer, so it all came easier to them. Jamie felt the power surge up her arms and encircle her hands. The raw energy stung as it clung to her fingers, and her splayed fingers tightened into claws as she let the joy of that stinging take her. She embraced it all, balancing on the razor's edge. Her ruby light sparked against the jade, turning from crimson to magenta. She breathed out a steady breath, letting her lungs empty completely, and then letting them empty some more.

Jamie watched her hands as she breathed back in, and the lightning dancing along her hands caught fire. The flames of red began to crackle within each hand. She stood, arms out, ready to be crucified as the deepening red flames waved and danced against the green wind. The flames were a step down in intensity from the electricity, as if it had been muted somehow. The feeling changed—still powerful, but hollow, an echo of what it had been in its raw and wild form. She could feel it now, the ability to shape it and make what she needed.

She framed an image in her mind and pushed the flame to take shape. And yet the flame still crackled and danced, unchanged by her push. She closed her eyes and put the image she wanted at the fore, and she pushed. She pushed like a woman trying to give birth, and she could feel the sweat begin to form on her forehead. But still, the flames crackled and danced. The others had made it look so easy, yet with all her might, she could not force the shape to form.

She quieted her mind and looked at what she had done. It

was a shape she held, but not a shape she wanted. Force had done nothing to help. But what had Alex said? Embrace, focus. The very essence of Uazit was rebellion from control. It was Uazit's power; it would not succumb to force. Jamie let these thoughts pass through her mind as she felt the flames dance and the world turn. She accepted them, and she let go of the image she had created and allowed the power to take her mind, take her body.

She embraced it, and as she did, the flames began to harden and cool. Within her hands, she held two ruby daggers, long and sharp. The power burned through them, and they hurt to hold. But it was a good hurt, the hurt of the power. She began to laugh as she looked at what she held. And then she began to dance. She had no conscious thought of dancing. No need or plan; her body just began to move. It whirled and plunged, first down then up, in a graceful spinning that took her from one end of the clearing to another. She cut through the jade light as she passed, leaving tracers of red like tomato in guacamole. Jamie had always liked to dance, but this was new; this was movement with total freedom from all thoughts and feelings. It was the beauty of the now filling her with, and fulfilling, a desire she could barely understand. But she moved, that is all she knew.

The laughter and chatter of the others dimmed and then

stopped. Jamie was unsure if they watched in silence or joined in, or if she merely no longer needed to hear them. But she danced, faster and faster, in flips and spins that brought life to her cells and fire to her breath. She danced until she collapsed in a heavy-breathing sigh of joy and contentment. And as her light puttered out, she saw it had been the last light of the day. The rainbow light of her team was gone. The others sat around where she lay upon the earth, and the sun beat down upon them from the west. It had been morning lessons when she had started. Had she danced, embraced in power, all day?

When Jamie had stopped breathing so hard and had begun to pay attention, Alex was shaking his head as if to a voice only he could hear. His eyes seemed to see a point well beyond the clearing and his students. He watched something, shook his head as if to disagree, then bowed in acquiescence. The other students sat quietly, practicing small, intricate forms built from their power. Jamie's outburst of dance, it seemed, had largely been ignored.

Alex looked at the team and sighed. "Each of you has been working hard. You live here in isolation, having only each other. This is all good, but it is unhealthy if it lasts for too long, unbroken. And so, a break is in order. The break will come at a cost, though. To go, you must learn to Travel." Alex seemed to pronounce the word with a capital letter.

"You will go as a team, and as a team you will return. Neither I nor Hempel will accompany you. Today, you will spend what little day that is left in contemplation and rest. Tomorrow, before the rising of the sun, you will Travel. A destination must be picked and agreed upon by the team. You will spend the day doing what you wish, surrounded by the noise of other people.

"Hempel suggests something close, yet different in look and feel. The wilds of Idaho are the perfect place for me. Their wild beauty is unparalleled in all the world. But Hempel reminds me that any sight gets tiresome when it is all you see. This is especially true for young eyes, I imagine. Think, children, and decide the location of your break." With that, Alex rose from the ground and walked away.

The buzz of excitement filled the air and followed the group the rest of the day. Jamie realized quickly that the others had interpreted "contemplation and rest" to mean argument and gossip. Suggestions of towns and locations were spread out for debate and cast into potentials and failures. A nonstop barrage of noise filled them. They agreed it would be unfair to visit one family. That kicked out Chicago, Seattle, Toronto, Mexico City, and Honolulu.

They decided to honor Hempel's guidance and stay within

a close radius of Coeur d'Alene. Portland was nixed, as only Russ liked strippers and nobody liked hippies. Missoula sounded nice, but most of Montana sounded like the same pine trees and mountains they had here. Nobody liked the idea of Boise, but mostly because none of them knew anything about the city. That went for the states of Utah and Wyoming as well. California could be nice, but then, as Russ pointed out, they were getting farther away. Really, at that point, only one viable option remained. Las Vegas. None of them had been, and it sounded awesome. A day of gambling—get a drink, steal a car, have a fling—all the things they each had enjoyed before coming to the school.

Once that had been decided, it was already night, and Jamie lay upon her bed, looking out over the trees, into the stars. The stars shone bright in a way they never had in the city. She could make out each bright speck like it was sitting close enough to touch. She traced the Milky Way from one side of the window to the other. A river of light filling her eyes with oranges, blues, and whites. It was a thing she had only seen in photos before coming here. Even with the glass between her and it, this was like no photo she had ever seen.

Joe sat at her desk, looking at the laptop, while Nettle lay sprawled out on the couch, reading off a tablet. They had wondered together what Traveling meant and what it was like.

They had debated and guessed for almost an hour before falling into silence. It was companionable silence to Jamie, and the company was welcome for it. Joe and Nettle had seemed to adopt her as part of a clique within the group. Whether this was due to Jamie actually being likable or María's completely anti-social attitude when it came to dealing with others and Russ' frequent lack of interest in anything but lifting and video games, she did not know. But it was nice to have companions in her life. With that thought and the beauty of the stars, Jamie slipped into sleep. The warmth of Nettle so close was a comfort, and Joe a friendly, safe energy at the desk made her feel warm. She slept, content and happy to be surrounded by creatures like her.

The next day, well before morning, there was a mass of movement. All of them were expected to be up and ready in time to go. They were given packs with whatever odds and ends the adults thought they needed, which seemed to include a few treats Alex had made, bottled water, money, IDs, and cellphones with each other's numbers and the numbers for Alex and Hempel preprogrammed in. Alex was like an old mother hen, going over each of them from head to foot to ensure they were ready, all while Hempel stood to the side, arms crossed and looking cross.

It did not take long before they were deemed ready and led out to the clearing where they had practiced their power the day before. Alex stood before them, hands clasped in front of him. He looked to Hempel, then sighed and looked at the students.

"Traveling is a use of the power to physically get from here to there. There are faster nonphysical methods, but today you Travel. It is easiest to perform. The power will surround your body and lift you up and set you down where you want to go." With that, Alex flourished his hands around him, and the green lightning covered him in shining zigzagging lines that crossed and re-crossed around him until it looked like a cocoon of green light encapsulated him. A deep hum began in the air of the clearing, and it purred deep in Jamie's chest as she watched the power surge around Alex. The jade cocoon lifted into the air and sat there. The light grew brighter and brighter. And then it was gone, and Alex stood a few feet away, back upon the ground, absent of light. The sudden change was a darkening of the world after so much light.

"The power will envelope you. The more you do it, the faster you will become. Little can penetrate the shielding once it is in place. It cuts you off from the world and moves you, but do not rely on it for safety. You must guide the Travel.

"Embrace your power. Focus it on a single point of light, all of it on that one point before your eyes. A solitary moment of existence lives within that moment. Move the point around you like an electron around an atom. Let it spin and spin, orbiting you in new shapes. It will weave the web you need around you. Once it begins to cover you, open your mind to all that power. Let it fill you; let it consume you; do not focus it on any one part of you. It must be allowed to live and breathe on its own.

"Once it has filled you and covered you, rise and go. Imagine your destination and let your body move there. As you Travel, you will see the world around you. Your ability to change direction and move around will help you to safely reach your destination or find a new one on the way.

"You may begin." Neither Alex nor Hempel had moved a muscle while he spoke. They merely watched the team. After he had stopped talking, the two continued to make no movement; the adults just stood. A stillness overcame them as they stood witness. The moment had come for the team to take their next step.

Jamie stood straight and let the power fill her. The rubies at her throat began to pulse. The power pulsed like long, thin breaths. In and out. First shallow then deeper. A warm deepening filled her. She was the well it filled. The sponge that soaked up all that pain. It filled her deeper and deeper. It became her and solidified what she was.

She focused that power into a single point of light in front of her. It hurt to hold it there. It hurt to watch the light first spark then grow. A deep crimson light that floated in the air before her. She was that point, just as she was her body. As she focused on the light, she continued to feed it. It drank in the power. It drank in her. But as she fed this point, the power within her did not diminish. Instead, it grew. A torrent of electrical impulses fed her mind and body a constant stream of light. And she allowed the point to move.

It moved with a whiplash of speed that seemed to crack the air around her. At first, it created circles of traced light around her head and then began to move down and up her body. The tracers began to weave in and out of each other, connecting to each other. The fabric of woven light blanketed her. Each intersection was a new spark on her skin—like fire. And soon, no part of her body did not burn with the joy of it. She laughed, for every spark only grew the power within her. This is what getting struck by a million bolts of lightning must feel like, she thought as her entire body shook.

The cocoon that formed embraced her and sank down around her skin like a second layer of life. The point of light that had been spinning stopped as quickly as it had begun. It rested at the peak of the cocoon, right above her head. It pulsed with the rubies at her throat. And the pulse slowed until it was a single light, a beacon that drew her eyes. As she focused, she imagined the fountain by the Bellagio. They had agreed to meet there.

The power flexed around her. Jamie had always wanted to fly. Wondered what it was like to be Superman. This was nothing like flexing a muscle. It was not a jump or an effort. It was simply falling. She focused on that point of light above her, and she began to fall towards it. Gravity had changed its point of reference for her.

As a child, Jamie had once jumped from the highest diving board in the local pool. The feeling of adrenalin as she had fallen weightless had filled her with a wild joy. The rising of the wind had crawled up her spine and tingled along her neck. She had hit the water too soon. The joy was there and gone in a second. But this fall, it lasted. The sky called out to her as she tumbled up into the stars. The sky embraced her, and she felt a wild abandon greater than anything she had ever known.

How far she fell she could not tell. But at some point, she felt the pull to the south. Her point of light moved from its peak and settled down before her eyes. The point turned her toward the edge of the world, and she began to fall in a whole new direction. She began to fall toward the skyline in a dizzying speed of adrenalin. The morning light dimmed the stars as she tumbled into the morning.

How long she fell or how fast she could not tell. But eventually, she stopped somewhere above a cityscape with buildings of awe-inspiring size. The sheer magnitude of what had been built below her gave her pause. Humans had this need to change the world around them and leave their mark. This was a testament to the egos of all who had been here. It was beautiful to Jamie, life-affirming.

She had learned a limited ability to guide her path. And she slammed against the pavement on a sidewalk next to a fountain. The feel of the ground striking her feet drove her to her knees. There was a moment of jarring impact as the cocoon of light around her drained away. Jamie's power left her alone and hollow. The pulsing that filled her was an ache compared to the voracious life she had known only moments before. She sighed at the loss and then stood and looked around. Nettle stood before her, smiling her little smile as the others began to land around her. Multicolored falling stars striking the ground in a single spot. They came to rest with a harsh slap, and the ground shook slightly at their downfall. Jamie's team was beautiful, as they stood up and looked toward the fountain.

The buzz of people was overwhelming, after the silence of the mountains. There were thousands of them, and they crowded around the team like bees around a flower. Jamie could see why. Her teammates were beautiful people, dressed in beautiful clothing. She had always known it, from the first moment she had seen them. But this was different; this was seeing them around other people. How much brighter they shone than all others. They were racehorses standing amongst nags. Jamie felt a surge of pride that this was her group.

The excitement in her team's eyes filled her with joy, and she felt an answering excitement in her own. They began to walk the Strip. Taking in sights, enjoying the way people looked at them. Enjoying the life around them. It filled Jamie with a buzz that echoed in the power within her. The power seemed to feed on the attention people showed her. She drowned in it for a moment and then was raised on the waves of humanity.

It was a glorious feeling. And they danced through the streets. They learned they were too young to do almost anything inside the casinos, so they merely enjoyed the crowd. The stores and restaurants were themed and beautiful and tacky all at once. The sun was hot, and the streets were long. It took most of the day to go even halfway across the Strip. The distance between buildings was part of the reason, but the constant need to stop and look took much of its own time. They backtracked at every corner and laughed as they followed random crowds and took whimsical side trips.

They found themselves outside the Diablo about the time they were hungry, and Russ was adamant that they should give it a try. María was unsure how "real" the Mexican food would be but was willing to give it a chance. The rest did not really care, so they went up the stairs to grab a bite.

Halfway up the stairs, a man in a suit grabbed Joe's arm and threw him against the railing. The man's suit was impeccable and tailor-fit. It was a shiny charcoal material with a matching vest and tie. The white shirt seemed to glow under such a dark suit. The man's smile came from a classically handsome face framed in dark black hair, cut military-short. The man stepped back and lifted his arm, a sheathed sword outstretched.

His features seemed Arabic to Jamie. His suit and stance screamed high-class professional. Everything about him looked as if it had been painstakingly perfected in front of a mirror only minutes before. His hair was short but stylish. He was clean-shaven and had a practiced look of elegance, the suit unrumpled and tailor-fit. His shoes even shone in the sunshine, and the sword's sheath looked polished. Jamie could not help but giggle at the thought that this man made the street he stood on a higher class of street.

"Who the hell are you?" Nettle stood suddenly ready as

she addressed the man. The team was randomly scattered along the stairs, and they moved as one, turning to face this threat. Jamie had been unsure that the constant drilling was working, but the way they moved was as a unit. The man stood stock-still. If he was unnerved by facing four teens, he showed no sign of it. As Joe climbed back to his feet, the number became five. The man still just stood, sheathed sword held out. Jamie could hear María breathe a sigh of relief as Joe regained his footing, and she moved closer to cover him. The boy was the youngest, and everyone treated him like a younger brother.

Jamie felt the rubies at her neck begin to pulse more deeply, and she drew in the power. It filled her as she prepared for the next step. She cycled quickly through the raw energy— into flame and out on the other side, with knives in her hands. She moved in closer, following Nettle's lead.

"Did they not tell you about me? I am Carlisle. And I have been waiting years to finally meet the Chosen of Uazit. Raven's were such a disappointment." He moved like a striking viper. The air cracked like a whip as he stepped in and swung his still-sheathed sword, only to have it blocked by the blade Nettle had pulled from her power. Nettle and Carlisle moved like lightning strikes—dancers moving, one and then the other, as they circled and weaved along the stairs. Jamie had not realized how fast

Nettle was, but this was who she really was; her mask was off. The strikes came hard and fast; the two spun and dodged. But as quick as Nettle was, Carlisle seemed faster. He blocked each blow and turned it back as quickly as it was struck. It was a dance of masters, but Carlisle seemed to have the upper hand. Nettle would have died had he unsheathed his sword.

The team moved, working in unison. Carlisle backed off at first, overcome by the onslaught. But once he got his footing, he struck back, step by step. He was a master, dodging in and out between each strike, waltzing from one person to the other. No blow touched him, and the team only avoided being struck by luck and speed. This one man moved through the entire team like it was grass waving in the wind. Jamie felt like she was pushing herself to her limit as she bent backward under the man's sword swing, but both this man Carlisle and Nettle seemed barely to be breaking a sweat.

Carlisle dodged back down the stairs onto the sidewalk and moved quickly away. As he did, inhuman warriors dressed in loose-fitting matching grey uniforms poured out into the midst of the team. Jamie found herself charged by a middle-aged man who came at her like a shot. She stepped into the charge as Hempel had trained her. Moving past the man, she drove her knife into his back on the way by. Turning swiftly, she sliced first in one direction and then in the other, letting blood flow. She moved from him into a second warrior who swung a sword at her. She rolled under the swing and flicked her knife into his ribs as she came up next to him and drove her other knife into his neck. She leaped back, pulling her knives with her as blood sprayed after her.

She could see the team in action. Russ had thrown a man completely down the stairs and followed that by driving a dark blue ax into the head of another. María threw bolts of golden light directly into the hearts of those who came too close, driving them back and then down. Jamie saw María place her hands upon the head of a kneeling woman and smile as golden light poured from the woman's eyes, burning them away, as her screams first rose and then quieted. María was a golden goddess in need of a worshiper. Joe seemed to use some sort of staff of ivory light too bright to look upon to drive back an assailant. The light flared whiter than an angel making a house call, blinding the entire stairway. As the light died, the man's head hit the stairs a few feet from his body. Nettle stepped back into a fray of her own opponents, moving like a swath through grass.

Jamie stood breathing one breath after the other, looking at the living creatures she had turned into bodies in a matter of seconds. There had been no dance, just the straightforward charge driving into this moment. Where Nettle moved with grace, Jamie had merely moved forward. She had not thought about a single move; she had just reacted. She breathed and saw that her team had dropped the rest of the warriors on the stairs.

There was a certain level of shell shock on everyone's faces—shell shock and exhilaration. Everyone except Nettle, who looked beautiful and relaxed at the top of the stairs. Like every warrior queen before her, she looked as if this was her place in the world. Bodies and blood pooled at her feet as her obsidian sword shone under the sun. Jamie followed Nettle's gaze to the bottom of the stairs, where Carlisle stood clapping, surrounded by more warriors.

"You do not disappoint, children." He pulled his sword up and began to unsheathe a dark metal blade. He and his warriors stepped forward.

"Move, now. Five-point draw." With those words, Nettle broke a dam. The team retreated up the stairs, breaking like waves around her as she stood staring down at Carlisle. Jamie moved like the rest, backing up behind Nettle, leaving space between the team and the warriors at the bottom of the stairs, taking her position in the formation that Nettle had commanded. Jamie could feel the power growing within her as the team members stepped close to each other, in a strictly defensive posture.

"Travel, now. Home." The tone of Nettle's command brooked no comment, and the entire team began to prepare their power to Travel. Jamie could see warriors pouring up the stairs as the power began to encircle and envelope her. Before anyone could come close to her, she had tumbled up into the air like a ruby comet speeding into the sky. From her perch in the sky, she could see her teammates spiraling up after her, and together they circled into the sky before falling their way home.

On the trip back, Jamie's mind was filled with the memory of the assault. She played back the feel of her knives striking flesh. The feel of bodies falling around her and blood hitting her face. As her feet struck ground at home, she could not help but think the war had become real. And with that thought, she could not help but smile.

COMING TO TERMS

Jamie stood up straight after her landing and felt a bit of pride in the fact that she had touched down first. The rest of the team came in after her landing one by one, starting with Nettle. She felt a bit of disappointment that Nettle's landing seemed smoother than hers, but she held onto the fact that she had been faster. Speed sacrificed a little control; everyone knew that. She would never get tired of watching her team touch down in a rainbow of falling fire.

She could feel the blood of those she had fought like dry glue on her face and hands. Her clothing was spackled in it. Evidence of her world changing. She needed a shower. The clearing was bright and sunny—so strange to find such peace after the storm of action they had just left. Jamie felt a pang of disappointment over that. The thrumming inside her almost wept. Her hands ached to hold her daggers.

Jamie was surprised to see Alex and Hempel standing in the clearing, waiting for them. There was a buzz of activity as the team attempted to explain what had happened to a confused Hempel and a contemplative Alex. They were obviously still amped on the excitement of what had occurred. Words tumbled out like leaves from a bucket. Jamie was slightly saddened. Amid combat, she had seen her team members' true faces, and here she was seeing the masks pulled back over the creatures they were. Their humanity covered their truth.

Joe seemed shaken as words poured out of him. Explaining about the guy with a sword and the fight that had ensued on the stairs, he kept spinning his words around, dropping out bits and pieces without any real attempt at chronological order or even any real sense. In his nervousness, he kept jumbling the story up and picking out the brightest pieces of the yarn. He got most of the main points, though, and his words flowed like a river rapidly hammering over rocks and rapids. Jamie was content to let him tell the story while she thought things through.

Russ pitched in here and there, throwing in the tale of how he had hurled someone like a rag doll. From his description, he had held off an army. An ancient Viking of lore retelling the great raid. From the blood splattered against his chest and the streak of it along his cheek, darker than his red hair, it was a believable interpretation. He swung his arms around to punctuate his tale and reenact his memory of what had happened. His boisterous words and pantomime made for an interesting performance. Between the two boys, most of what had occurred was colorfully, if confusingly, told.

"There were so many of them; they just kept coming. Just so many."

"Eleven less." María's quiet statement was deadpan, and the boys' excitement was noticeably absent in her words. A moment of stillness amid their chaos.

"What?"

"There are now eleven less." María smiled and said nothing else, but Jamie could see the girl drawing in her power and watching it dance around her hands. She seemed serene. She was the pinnacle of exquisiteness. Whatever she felt about what had happened, the ice princess kept it inside. She looked like a Bodhisattva finally reaching enlightenment. The golden glow of her power only added to the tranquil beauty on her face. If there was excitement from the fight, she had let it go. All sense of agitation or worry was absent. Her look said that the conversation was unimportant; she had chirped in just to add a fact. She was the most content of them all.

Nettle looked bothered, though, and that worried Jamie. Nettle stood looking at the team and then at the teachers, then back at the team. She met Jamie's eyes, and Jamie really took in her leader's features. The girl's hair was wild and unkempt. She had moved quickly through the fight, and everything about her seemed tangled. Yet the wildness looked strangely right on her. Having only ever seen Nettle as the image of unplanned perfection, it was a new look. The soft kitten was gone, and steel stared out from her eyes. Those eyes were on Alex, and they did not seem sure of what they saw.

Jamie recalled her thoughts on the stairs—that this was Nettle's true face. And here, with the time to drink in the details of blood splatter and obvious recent exertion, Jamie realized how right she had been. Nettle was a warrior queen, an ancient amazon. Her flirty, flighty act had been pulled away—a cover for a warrior that stood tall in the face of death. Nettle had spent the day doing what she had been built for. It was beautiful and terrifying to behold. She was beautiful and terrifying to behold. Jamie envied her the easy acceptance with which she faced her life. But still, Nettle was bothered, and her words cut through the boys' recital like a knife through butter.

"This man—he said his name was Carlisle."

The sharp intake of breath from Hempel silenced the

group. She glanced quickly and irritably at Alex, who still stood contemplatively, and then her eyes looked straight at Nettle. Hempel spoke in a breathy rush. "He had a sword. This man—he carried a sword."

Alex touched her arm as if to calm her. Then he, too, looked at Nettle. It had, up until now, been the first movement he had made since they had returned. He followed it with the first word he had uttered. "Describe."

"Yes, he had a sword. It was sheathed, most of the fight. The sheath was black. Horn, by the feel of it, and the glow. When unsheathed, it was metal, but a dark smoky metal. It was like night and stars shining in his hands. The quality was the best I have ever seen. The man looked mildly Arabic or East Indian. I cannot be sure. He was well-dressed—one of the fanciest suits I have ever seen. He fought..." Nettle paused, as if remembering how easily he had danced among the entire team's attacks. Remembering how it had felt to strike and parry and feel the weight of loss looming. "He fought as a master swordsman. I have never faced the like. Forgive me, mistress, but I think he would have challenged even you. The others with him were good. It was obvious they had been trained. We were better. They had numbers. I did not get a count as I should have. But María is correct; there are eleven less of them."

"It is true, then. He still uses the Raven Sword." Hempel looked stricken, her eyes drilling into Alex as if willing him to speak. She looked irritated with him, and this irritation mixed with her obvious agitation in a way that made her appear almost antsy.

Alex had returned to his contemplative look. He stared back into Hempel's eyes for minutes that felt like hours before his body relaxed and he sighed. His words were like a whisper closing around the throats of everyone there. "It and his life will be removed from his possession if I have to cut off his hand with a spoon to get it." The oddly phrased promise slipped along the air and out into the world. Hempel noticeably relaxed as she looked at Alex and he at her. There was no other debate to be had. The level of trust of between one human being and another was apparent in her reaction.

******

The team was expected to shower and clean up and report to the dining room. Jamie struggled to peel off her clothing, sticky with blood and sweat. Her belief that it had all dried was shown to be a lie, as her hand seemed to find a wet mess everywhere she tried to grab. Jamie could remember once falling into mud on her way home and how she had felt cleaner as it dried—until she had tried to get her clothing off and breaking open the cracks of mud had revealed slime still wet underneath. This was the same, and the same greasy feeling came over her now, as it had then, when she looked at the naked woman in the mirror.

Blood was in her hair and dried along her skin. It looked like someone had thrown a bucket of red paint at her that she had been helpless to dodge. But she looked calm, to her own eyes. Slightly irritated by the level of clean-up that awaited her, but she was calm. Not the perfect serenity of María or the fierce beauty of Nettle. But her own stoic calm that said she was ready. And in that calm, Jamie could see a glint of her own attractive features that rivaled the other two women in intensity, if not appearance.

She would always envy them their grace and stylish manners, but there was something to be said for direct action without flourish. There was the beauty of a knife cutting through the noise. And the woman in her mirror had that beauty. For once in her life, she understood that her lack of stereotypical womanly wiles was just a difference, and not a lack. How she was and what she did had value. She had put down two attackers, while the rest of the team had still been figuring out what was going on. She could see things the way they really were, because she did not dress up her reality in frills and lace. What was there was what she saw.

The woman in the mirror was beautiful and valuable to the world around her. But that did not really matter, because more importantly, she was beautiful and valuable to herself.

She climbed into the shower, leaving the bloody mess of fabric on the floor, and let the hot water pour down over her in wave after wave of warmth. The water washed away more than the grime that covered her. It washed away a tension she had not even known she carried inside. The events of the day began to feel alien and far away. The memories of someone else's life that Jamie had merely observed in a movie or a book. The water washed over her and into the drain. The feelings she had nearly felt washed down with it.

The shower was long and yet over too quickly. She toweled off and started to sort clothing for dinner. She needed relaxed and comforting clothing. She threw on black sweat pants and a red hoodie. Her father had taken her, as a child, out running with him, and he always wore his hoodie and sweat pants to do it. He claimed he got too cold in shorts and a t-shirt, after a day wearing a uniform. He kept his t-shirts for inside the house. He had spoken of his hoodie like it was armor, protecting him against the cold world outside. Jamie felt a comfort, a normalcy, in mimicking his look. It was her armor for the conversation that was to come.

The dining room was a long, narrow room with wooden walls. If it had been in a movie, chandeliers would have hung from the ceiling, and a long, narrow table would have filled the room with glowing wooden light. But here, lights, like antique streetlights, were affixed to the walls. Their spacing and height seemed to be at random intervals along the wall, as if someone had just nailed them in place where they happened to find them. The room was oddly comforting, and the large, square table they ate at was askew toward the door, leaving the rest of the long room empty. The asymmetrical setup had actually discomforted Jamie the first few times she had eaten in here, mainly because she had never seen a purpose for so much leftover space on the one side. The room was cozy, though in a completely jumbled way. Of all the rooms in the house, this one felt the most jarring because of the builder's inability to follow any real design plan while still making a room that was easy to enjoy.

The others were already sitting at the table, munching on finger foods and talking, when Jamie came in. One look at the food and she realized she had not eaten, except for a snack here or there, since before dawn. What with all the Traveling, exploring, and killing, she suddenly realized she was ravenous. She charged the table and had a plate almost full and a huge bite in her mouth before she had taken a seat.

She met María's eyes and realized that the girl had a daintily held fork in one hand and a small piece of fish on her plate. Her demeanor was stiff, and the look she gave Jamie screamed that if eyerolling was not ill-mannered, she would have been rolling hers with vehemence at such barbaric behavior. Jamie smiled back sheepishly and closed her mouth to slowly and quietly finish chewing her mouthful. María's eyes could judge you, even as her posture made clear that making judgments was beneath her. How difficult it must be to know how the world should act, but those good manners meant you were unable to ensure it acted that way.

Jamie weighed this odd understanding of María as they ate in silence and the others around them filled the air with chatter. She could not help it as she whispered across the table, "Maybe you need a little savage in you, Princess." María gave her a small smile and went back to her fish.

Alex sat at one corner of the table, still looking as if a puzzle that only he could see rested in the air. He was quiet when he spoke, as if his words had a volume of their own, and he did not wish to add to it by speaking them too loudly. "Uazit called to all of you today, and you answered. You know now what you must do. You know what you must do with the power she has given you. That power is a negotiation with our Queen. She is not a tyrant to rule you. She gives and she takes, and you must agree upon the price of the deal to be struck. Some prices are subtler then others. I had hoped we had years yet to teach you. We do not. They found you at the moment you left the safety of our home. This means the time is gone for you to be innocent. You have tasted the war. We must progress. I have asked Hempel to show you the dangers of what could be. You must learn your duty."

He was quiet then. He turned, as if he had forgotten his own speech, and began to think again about whatever puzzle had so fascinated him. The room sat eating in silence. A few kept looking at Hempel as if waiting for her to talk. They sat until darkness filled the windows and the light of the day had died. Hempel stood then and told them she had a story to tell them. Quietly, the group stood up and followed her out the door.

Once outside, Hempel picked up the pace to a light jog. They followed a trail through the trees for a while, on their silent run, but at a spot that looked like any other, Hempel veered off into the tangle of brush and trees. The team followed. They ran into the night, under the stars. It was a purity of movement through that darkness. Jamie could breathe in the fresh air of the deep forest, and she realized how much she loved these woods.

The night air whipped past her as she dodged branches

and jumped fallen timber. She clambered up rocks and slid down hills of grass and weeds. Hempel ran ahead of her, and Jamie did her best to stay close. The group spread out behind Jamie as they struggled to keep up. Nobody was left behind, but nobody else came close to catching her. The pure scent of pine filled her nostrils as she breathed deep and pushed harder. They ran for hours in silence until they met a river, where they stopped. Three canoes lay out on the banks, and a fire crackled near a stand of trees.

Under the trees and near the river, a mound of blankets and skins sat next to the large bonfire. The mound looked like a large bowl flipped over, with an entrance on one side; blankets hung loose along the edge to pull over the small doorway. Towels were piled near benches, around the fire.

As soon as she stopped running, Hempel began to undress. Jamie watched as Alex and Nettle, finally catching up, began to do the same. The other kids came in, minutes later, breathing hard and taking in the scene as they rested. They stood watching for a few minutes before Russ and then María began to undress as well. Jamie felt her cheeks flush but soon followed suit, removing her clothing until she stood naked under the stars. She assumed Joe was also doing the same, but she dared not look. She hoped they did not look at her, either. It was one thing to see herself as beautiful, alone in her bathroom, and another thing to show herself off to the entire group.

The heat of the fire pushed against her front as the cold wind of the night beat at her back. She looked at the ground, trying to ensure she made eye contact with no one, and was extra careful that her eyes also contacted nothing else. She had not felt this uncomfortable in a long time. She kept telling herself that it was just bodies, and it was not like they did not all have the internet. But it did not matter; her nervousness about her own nudity was still too fresh.

She jumped at a tap on her shoulder and turned to see Nettle holding out an old, worn towel, a small mischievous smile on her face. The girl was trying to look adult and serious, but the glint of humor ruined it. Jamie did not care what Nettle thought and mimed thank you, unable to find her voice. She then turned quickly back to looking at the fire as she could see that Nettle's own towel was uncaringly thrown over a shoulder. Her naked body looked lithe and firm, outlined by the fire's flickering light. Jamie wrapped her towel around herself in a true example of speed. All thoughts of nudity or nervousness were driven out of her head like wheat separating from chaff as sound filled the space around her.

A deep, long note of sorrow escaped from Hempel's throat

as she began to sing. The song was more feeling and sound than words or phrases, but it was all meaning. Alex used a pitchfork to dig bright red rocks from the fire and deposit them into a hole inside the mound. Hempel motioned the teens to follow her as she turned and entered the mounded structure on her hands and knees, moving backward into the darkness. The song never wavering in its beauty. If anything, it echoed louder and filled the night. Single file, they followed her. All had to crawl through the small opening, and all of them followed her lead in entering backwards. For a second, as her feet were in and her head faced out, Jamie felt panic at what she might be backing into. But once inside, she found herself sitting between Joe and Nettle, staring at the small opening of light as Alex reached out and pulled blankets down to cover the entrance.

They sat in the darkness, naked and warm. The water hitting the rocks crackled and steamed, filling the air with heat and damp. Jamie found it harder and harder to breathe, as the steam continued to build and the heat began to burn her face and hands. She kept sitting up, staring at where she thought Hempel sat. The teacher sang and spoke a language that Jamie had never heard yet felt the pull of in her heart.

The woman switched to English and spoke of giving thanks to all things in their lives. The mothers and grandmothers who had raised them and cared for them, teaching them the way of their world. She thanked the wives and female lovers who had comforted and cared for them. She thanked the sisters and friends who had looked out for them and protected them. The air kept getting hotter, until Jamie thought she might pass out from the sheer heat of it. Who knew it was so hard to breathe in damp air? Just when she thought she could take no more, Hempel solemnly ended with "all our relations," and they exited.

The night air was cold on Jamie's skin. In imitation of the others she walked over to the river and jumped in, feeling the cold water wash away the sweat and heat she had built up inside. She used a deep bowl she found on the bank to pour the water over her face and body and take large drinks. She had never been so thirsty, and the water was like crystal joy on her tongue. Bathing in the river froze her, but this was what she had seen everyone else do and assumed it was correct. She felt the sacredness of this moment and did not wish to get it wrong through ignorance. After washing, she grabbed her towel and joined the others by the fire.

The fire was huge and crackling, and everyone around her smiled and laughed as they told stories and jokes. Jamie was quiet. What was appropriate and what was not? She did not know, so she just listened. Alex had rolled a cigarette and was gently smoking. He rolled another and handed it to Nettle, who smiled and took it from him. After a time watching the fire, they went back into the structure.

Hempel poured water onto the rocks as Jamie sweated and stared at the darkness. It was getting easier to breathe in the heat and damp, yet Jamie knew that she could not survive a long stint in this heat. She did her best, though, and sat tall as the water hissed and the world seemed to wait.

Hempel sang again and gave thanks to all the men in their lives. The fathers and grandfathers who had protected them and looked out for them. The fathers who helped raise them and love them. The brothers who had looked out for them and tricked them into bad behavior. The lovers and husbands who had held them safe and provided when it was needed. She gave thanks for Alex by name and all he had done to teach the children. And when her prayers were done, with a solemn remembrance of all their relations, they again exited the lodge and washed in the cold river and sat in towels around the fire. The cycle continued as they sat and smoked and laughed. Then, it was time to go back in.

This time, Hempel was talking to them as much as to the spirits. Her words came out as puffs and sighs rising in the darkness. "Grandmother, we thank you for these children that will wage our war with us. We give thanks for their strength and wisdom as they move forward. They will need it. As they face Order and try to save themselves and all your children from it, they will need that strength. That wisdom. Children, hear me. Hear the tale of the Raven's Chosen, so that you may learn from it.

"The man you saw and fought goes by the name of Carlisle. He is now a Champion of Order. Much like you are Uazit's Chosen, the Queen of Order chooses Champions to enact her will in the world. She lies and manipulates others into joining her side and fighting for her. She incorporates armies of inhuman soldiers into her machinations. Those armies follow the Champions. Carlisle and those like him have begun a massive shift in this war.

"My own family was Chosen by Raven. Carlisle and his like exterminated them, and now there is just me left to defy the Champions of Order. Raven did not give us collars like Uazit gives her Chosen. Instead, he created weapons of his own feathers, forged in the heat of his lust and cooled in his own blood, to give his children. Each weapon a symbol of perfect creation and lethal force. He worked upon the ice of the arctic for a generation before deciding the weapons were finished, and at that time he wept. He had made six to gift the world with freedom. The ulus, the sword, the spear, the blades, the bow, and the harpoon. The first six Chosen trained upon the ice, learning the many ways to use their individual weapon. The weapons were passed from one Chosen to another, generation after generation, each new user adding more knowledge before passing it on. Their use was taught from master to apprentice.

"We were separated into two-person teams. Master and student. Our master taught us everything we needed to know, and we used that knowledge to take up the war in their place once they died. Because of our one-on-one tutelage by the previous owner of our weapon, we did not form a fighting team such as you. It is true you each have unique powers through your individual collar, but our power was our weapon. And can you imagine the beauty of our forms? The might of lone warriors traveling from one side of the world to the other, finding and fighting the forces of Order. Wandering defenders of freedom. It made us a family, deeper than any blood.

"Raven's Chosen were the jewels of the Tricksters' army. The Chosen of other gods looked at us as the example all should follow in the fight to free the world from Order. One weapon-holder could turn the tide of an entire battle. We were the finest gems and sparkled as we cut through the formations of Order. My own master, Horace, holder of the Raven Ulus, taught me to take pride in our greatness. We were the strongest, preening upon the altar of our greatness.

"But it was not to last forever. Carlisle killed the master of the Raven Sword and took the sword for his own. He used it to slaughter, one by one, the master and apprentice of every weapon until it was only me. The ulus are sacred to the Raven, so Carlisle had saved me for last.

"We fought a fierce, unholy battle upon the sands of a desert I do not even remember the name of. What I remember is the heat of the sun above and the burning grit of the sand beneath. We circled like wild beasts under the hot noon sun. Our hatred for each other burned brighter and hotter than anything in the desert. We struck blows under the dawn that would have felled trees. We moved under the stars like flashes in the sky. The battle lasted days, and by the end, we were both wasted with hunger and thirst. That desolate place we scorched even worse, decimating the little life and stability that had existed. Under the falling sun, spraying hues of crimson and gold, Carlisle bested me, but I escaped. My throat still scratches from the thirst I felt as I buried myself in that desert.

"It was a harsh and unforgiving land. No water or food in sight. The heat of the day would bake my skin from my bones, while the frozen nights filled my dying eyes with stars so bright I could touch them. I spent weeks in the desert, slowly working my way to the edge. How Carlisle escaped the desert, with the cuts I left him, I do not know, but somehow, we both made it out.

"Before we had fought, I had called in a major debt owed to me by a renowned thief. She had used the time Carlisle fought against me to steal the weapons back and hide them away. All but the Raven Sword, as he carried it with him. This was my only victory—the return of the weapons. My greatest failure was not to return the sword.

"The death of my family is what caused Raven to ask Uazit to form you. Coyote has been swallowed up by a bottle and lost to an environmental issue. His Chosen fight on another front. The Fox is hidden away, and none can find her. Raven spoke to Coyote and then they spoke to your goddess. They knew that the Chosen of Raven are lost for a time in this world. And their fear of Order winning outweighs their fear of your goddess.

"Those you face have destroyed great warriors. There is no promise that you will defeat them, but you have tasted their blood, and the war is now upon you. Make peace with who you were and come to terms."

Jamie put her hand upon her mouth, and the taste of blood still lingered. The story Hempel had told had spun out in the darkness for her, as she imagined the sparks and speed of the fight within the desert.

She could not help, though, to think about the time in the clearing, after they had returned. Hempel had looked at Alex with irritability almost bordering on accusation. And Alex—Alex had been contemplative, but never once surprised.

RETRIEVAL OF DAYS

Jamie knew darkness and nothingness. To say she knew darkness and nothingness was not exactly correct. What can darkness know? What can nothingness know? The floating insubstantial nothingness did not know anything, really, yet darkness and nothingness was all it knew. It was all it had, all it could experience.

All around Jamie was darkness and nothingness. To say all around her was darkness and nothingness was not exactly correct. Can darkness be surrounded by darkness? Can nothingness be surrounded by nothingness? Staring up at a starless sky, can there be a body of nothing within the nothing? Or is it all one? A solid canvas.

Jamie was darkness and nothingness. She hovered there, dark in dark. She reveled in her nothingness. As she began to think, her universe began to change. The solid canvas began to take on shades within the nothingness, creating a beautiful painting of half-thought thoughts and the echoing of nearly forgotten voices. The sky was going from the darkest dusk into full night. The deep purples and dark blues of memory seeped in like a bruise upon her once-empty mind.

She could feel her body forming. It was a beacon of red light that slowly began to glow. In the darkness around her, she could feel the ignition of other beautiful lights. She was a star surrounded by a pulsar, giving birth to a sea of stars to join her. The sky was filled with the floating balls of light that sat serenely in the darkness, like floating candles on a still pond. Jamie could see the other lights around her, and they were beautiful. She looked upon them with joy and happiness.

In her eons of studying of the lights, she noticed that the stars were connected by a network of gossamer webbing almost too thin to see. It intertwined with each star before it reached out and touched another. The thin veins were almost invisible to the eye, yet they created a network of light that permeated the sky around them. It was beautiful and complete, filling the darkness with life and light.

It was not meant to last. Jamie saw a single star begin to fall. Flaming as it brought death into the world below it. She could hear it scream, see it try to remain afloat. But it fell to the ground with a solid impact of suffering. The first was followed by more. The stars closest to the planet beneath them were being pulled by a force the others did not feel.

It would have ended there, but the stars that plummeted pulled tight the webbing that connected them all. It began to pull the rest of the beings of light from their safe orbits. It was a chain reaction, like a fisherman pulling in a net. The ground sucked up the stars closest and through them, pulled the entire network toward its surface. Jamie watched as star after star spiraled toward the earth and then struck it in pinpricks of fire. They were bombs exploding in flashes of light and dust, leaving craters upon the soil. It was a starry death pockmarking the living planet's surface.

Jamie began to fear her own impact with the ground. Would it hurt to be tugged by the gossamer webbing? Like a piece of string tied to her soul, yanking it along. She had had stitches once, and the feel of the long threads being pulled through her skin was the closest image she could form.

Would it hurt to strike the ground? At what point of impact would she stop feeling the ground hammer into her? Would her world go black at the moment of impact, or would she feel the light of her body explode out into the world? She was unsure which thought sounded better.

She waited for the feel of the net pulling against her as she watched star after star hurtle to the ground, each pulling more and more of their number with them. It looked like a million bobbing balloons going over a waterfall. Each slowly dragged to the point of gravity before it tipped over that edge and plummeted to the rocks below. Their beautiful connection was killing them all. Soon the sky below her was filled with a million points of dying light and a smoking ruin as the last of the stars began their fall. And still she felt no pull.

Looking for the first time at herself, she saw that she had no gossamer strings wrapped around her. Their hooks had somehow missed her. She had been a lone star amongst a nebula of connected beings. And so the net would never catch her. She could safely watch the last star pulled to its fiery destruction. She was left alone in the sky.

As the last of the light sputtered and died out, Jamie was left in darkness. To say she was left in darkness was not exactly true. Can darkness be left within itself? She floated there, a leaf of memory gently floating upon a still pond at night. She let go of that memory and began to sink, darkness into darkness, nothingness into nothingness. As she sank, she was calmed and became serene. This sinking was tranquility, and the deeper she went into the darkness, the deeper she went inside herself.

Because that was what she was doing in her mind, diving deeper and deeper by letting her descent happen. And in the bottomless depths of her own mind, she awoke to the smell of fire and the taste of pine trees. The sounds of life and light surrounded her. She opened her eyes to take in that world she was in, but not connected to.

She lay upon the earth, surrounded by trees. Warmth gripped her from behind as she gripped it before her. A gentle trickling of moving water was somewhere off to her right as she opened her eyes. She had fallen asleep near the fire the night before. Her bare back was pressed against Nettle's body, and María was to her front. Their towels had been thrown over them for warmth. Nettle's arm lay gently around her, holding her. María lay curled before her, and Jamie's arms were around her. The scent of dark hair filled her nostrils as she breathed deep. The heat of the other girls against her was a nice reminder that not all connections were lost to Jamie. She was sandwiched between flesh that cared for her.

But she was awake now, and the time of dreams was over. She hefted herself to her feet and searched for her clothing. She quickly donned it and walked down to the river to take a drink of its ice-cold waters. Her body felt relaxed and healthy, in a way she could not have described if asked. Something about last night had cleansed her.

The others slowly began to rise and dress. Jamie noticed that Joe had dressed sometime in the night. She washed her face as Russ went from sleeping to diving naked into the river next to her, his muscular body vaulting up and over her to crash into the waves. She laughed at his hijinks but then moved back to the camp, letting him have his fun. He splashed and swam for a time, but once he realized nobody was joining him and, worse, nobody cared, he climbed back out and got dressed. The group packed the little that was there and climbed into the canoes to trek downriver. Jamie made a mental note that this spot was on the same river as the one that passed the house.

Paddling slowly down the river, Joe had a question. "Hempel, did we do that because you are Indian? Was it an Indian thing to do?"

She smiled back at him and set her oar against the edge of the canoe. "We did not, Joseph. My people are from Alaska, and the ceremony we performed is from the South. It is a thing I have learned in my long life as a way to give thanks to those around us. A way to focus the mind on those things that must be considered. In your life, you will learn many ceremonies and many ways. It is good to embrace those that have meaning for you. Own yourself and your ways; do not own others. We should not claim to own things that belong to others; we merely borrowed it for a night, to share what needed to be shared."

For the next several months, Hempel pushed their fighting skills to the limit as she trained them harder than ever before. Hempel's training made their muscles constantly sore, but they knew what they were fighting against now and nobody complained. Jamie learned that she was capable of accomplishing things with her body that would never have been possible before coming to this school. Her body strengthened and tightened into an athletic frame. Her quiet pride in her ability continued to grow as her skills sharpened. She could remember the first time she saw the six-pack forming in the mirror. The person she had been would never recognize this new Jamie who could throw a man from one side of the room to the other and throw a knife with precision and accuracy.

Alex still taught them no actual violence, but he did begin to teach them strategy and assessment. His avoidance of the violent nature of what they did seemed at odds with what he was teaching them to become. But what he did teach them, he taught to perfection. He would test their observation skills at random moments by telling them to describe a room or object they had just seen. He once gave Jamie a hard candy when she could recount everything about a room she had seen in a picture for only a few seconds. It had been a surreal moment as he laughed and twisted his fingers up, revealing the candy and dropping it into her palm.

He recited to them words from Sun Tzu, Alexander, Tran Hung Dao, and other tacticians. He would run beside them or have them work through various yoga and calisthenics forms, talking about assessing landscapes and the art of deceit. He would ramble on about the generals of the past and how they viewed the world.

One morning, after a long run, Alex took them all to a room off the main hall that contained four massive tables covered in small, realistic models of landscapes and cities. He directed them to small hand-painted model soldiers that were arranged along shelves at the back of the room. He then showed them books of rules about how to use the models to play games of war. He walked them through game after game, until he was sure they understood, at which point he set them loose against each other as he walked the room and pointed out mistakes on the positioning of units.

He drove them obsessively to pay attention to the placement of each individual soldier in regards to their squads, and their enemy. He may not have taught them how to fight, but he taught them how to think in a fight. How to approach as a unit. How to break off as a unit. The game became a daily part of their training and practice, as did Hempel's increased push for them to spar over and over, often in brutal displays of ability. Not a day finished without sore muscles and a contented sigh.

For Jamie, the best training, though, was with their power. They each had special skills that the others found difficult to mimic, but there was a broad level of basic skills they all shared. Jamie twice tried to form a sword like Nettle's, thinking it would be nice to have the reach a sword would give her. The creation of the sword was difficult, and the result felt odd in her hand. It was like she was holding the sword wrong, and no change of her grip would fix the feel of it. There was no way to get the right balance; everything felt out of place. So she let the sword go and went back to her daggers, feeling an immediate comfort in how they felt.

They practiced in the power daily, often teaching themselves and each other. Nettle showed them that she could jump from one spot to the next, disappearing in a flash of charcoal lightning, only for that lightning to strike a short distance away, leaving her standing in the new location. The others tried, and nobody else could seem to get it right. Jamie showed them her own ability to capture the moment between moments and felt a certain level of pride in the others' inability to do it at the same level or with the same ease. They laughed as they tried the skills of the others, either failing completely or creating a difficult-to-perform replication that did not seem to work nearly as well.

María attempted to teach them how she threw her power as she had against the warriors in Vegas. They all had a minimal ability to really use the power at a distance, but María's missiles of gold could cut through a stone at over fifty yards. Her ability to cast lightning straight from her hand was a beautiful golden display of power. Joe astonished them all when he both blinded Russ with a shocking flash of light and then he just up and disappeared. His voice had come from the air, but nobody on the team could spot him. He had used his power to become invisible. Russ did not seem to have much in regards to flash in the special skills department. What he could do, though, was use his power to amplify his own physical abilities. They all experienced this to a degree, and Jamie herself moved faster than sound when the power filled her. But Russ could lift a level of tonnage that would have awed the Hulk. What he lacked in flash he made up for in physical prowess.

With their power had come skills they had never learned before. The speed with which they soaked up Hempel's lessons defied any real logical ability. Their bodies had been conditioned for learning when they had put on the collars, and much of the practice seemed to be reminding their brains what their bodies had already learned.

Their time followed a pattern over the months. Two nights a month, Alex would disappear until the next day, saying nothing and asking nothing. Hempel spent her free time in the forests around them or in her room. Neither adult seemed to especially care what the teens did away from their lessons, as long as the adults were not personally disturbed. The teens were left to their own devices, which took on many forms of entertainment and conversation.

Joe and Nettle continued to spend lots of time around Jamie. They spent their free time on walks around the forest or sprawled out somewhere, each doing their own thing. Joe was usually on a laptop, and Nettle most often was reading from her tablet or from a book she had found here or there. Jamie did whatever felt right at the time—throw a ball in the air, ask the other two questions, or practice flipping knives. Mostly, though, she quietly cycled through her power, enjoying the feel of it building within her and then letting it go. Letting it build until the pain of it burned her and then holding it for as long a time as she could. She knew she was obsessed, but she really did not care. The power was a living thing she could not but love.

One morning Alex sat them in meditation to quiet their

minds enough for them to 'Listen.' Jamie heard the capital letter in the way Alex said the word. What they were supposed to be listening for, he did not say. Just to "release the sound within them and let the Sound be heard." Jamie sat cross-legged, staring out at the candle Alex had placed before her. The flame danced up, then down, before the wind pushed it to the left and then let it stand straight again. She was unsure what she was trying to hear, but Alex was adamant. "Shut it and understand," was his command. How to do either seemed a lesson he was not about to teach.

Jamie breathed in a deep breath. She let it back out and felt her power within her. It was the same raw, pulsating pain it always was. The same pleasure in a can she had opened that first night. The red glow of her power danced like the flame of the candle. It was mesmerizing, and she relaxed. Her thoughts seemed to drift away, unimportant as the flame, and her power undulated and spiraled. The only thing that mattered was the dancing flame of her power. But then, she saw something within the light.

There was a mask. A green jade mask shaped like a man's frowning face, and it rested upon a pedestal of white marble. Jamie could not see the room around her, but she knew it was filthy with grime, covered in age, coated in dust, frosted in time long neglected. Her inner voice was gone, and she was unsure who was thinking for her. The words weirdly welded together, though in a wasting fashion. The mask seemed to stare at her. It reproached her for leaving it here in this dirty place, where only it remained clean. It was obviously disappointed in her and yet lacked any real career path to get itself out. It was waiting on the sofa of centuries for her to come and bail it out.

As she considered the mask's face, red began to drip down upon it in a slow, steady stream. The blood seemed to soak into the jade, and the pedestal went from a stark white to a crimson red. Jamie was mesmerized by the slow drip, and it took her a minute to realize the mask's mouth was no longer in the shape of a frown; it was now laughing.

The image of laughter crashed down into Jamie's mind like an anchor hitting the sea. Her brain felt like it should be bleeding and her eyes like they should be ripped from her head. The image was gone as quickly as it had come. The other voice that had thought for her was gone, mostly. It had drained away, like a nice creamy gravy down the sink, and taken its weird metaphors and word choices with it. She was as sure of that as a chimp-munk was sure its banana Bibles were safely squirreled away.

Jamie shook her head and realized she was lying face down on the floor and her candle had been kicked or knocked a good distance away. She tried to hold onto the image of the mask, but every time she refused to let it go, some odd phrase would describe her world.

She let the memory slip away and pushed herself back to a sitting position. A massive headache beat down on her brain. Alex was looking at her as if seeing something new, and the rest of the team sat comfortably in their lotus positions. Jamie forced herself to reset into her own lotus and try to clear her mind and make sense of what had happened. Focus was hard to come by, and she found it difficult to get comfortable again. Luckily, the lesson seemed to end as Alex began to tap the floor before him in long, loud thumps that reverberated through the floor and into Jamie.

She looked up and saw that the others were looking up as well. Alex's words filled the space around them. "You must retrieve it, children. You must free it and bring it home."

Nobody seemed sure what he meant, but then, Jamie was often confused by the many things he had said. This seemed like something she was supposed to pay attention to, so she did. Alex stood and walked among them, stooping periodically to tap each on the forehead. When it was Jamie's turn, she felt the small yet forceful tap. A gong seemed to strike within her head. It reverberated down her spine and around to her belly button and just kept pushing back up to her throat. The left side of her neck began to burn as her ears continued to ring. And then it was over.

It felt like a hard spot had formed on the skin of her throat, and her fingers involuntarily went up to touch it. It felt like a callous, about the size of a dime, had formed in a perfect little circle right under her jaw. It was a slight lump but not noticeable until she pressed in on it. She whispered to herself, "Aw, shit. What is this?" As soon as she pressed, her teammates looked over at her in shock and confusion. She released the pressure and coughed.

"How did you do that?" María sounded confused and uncertain.

"Do what?"

"Speak into our minds? I heard you like you were standing right next to me."

Jamie was uncertain what she was talking about, but the whole team was nodding their heads. Alex looked at them all in silence, waiting. His teaching technique for some things seemed to follow a pattern of watching and letting them figure things out. Jamie pressed again on the dime-sized lump and cleared her throat loud enough to be heard. The whole class reached up to their own throats.

"Can you hear me?" Joe's quiet, whispered voice came out as if it was right next to Jamie's ear. She laughed, nodded her head to Joe, and looked at Alex in surprise. The voices of the team members began to flood her ears as they all tried it at once. It was unnerving and exciting. Jamie found that even with the cacophony of the others, she could easily hear the world around her. It was like the noises came from inside and so had no impact on her ability to hear.

Alex explained. "I needed you to be able to Listen. The quiet mind that can hear others will be a skill you can eventually access, but it was apparent that today was not your day to learn such a simple lesson. You must Travel, though, to gather an artifact we need, so our ability to communicate will be required. I have used a trick to create a system or network that will allow you to speak to each other and myself. You all seem to have picked up the basic method to communicate with the entire group. There are many ways to use this. You can, by concentrating, speak to just one person, or potentially you could pick just a few others. The ways to communicate over this network are many."

Alex then waited while they all practiced. It seemed easy enough to imagine Joe and speak only to him. It was a bit trickier but still not that difficult to speak with Russ and María but leave out the rest. Jamie thought about all the movies and TV shows she had seen that used a similar idea with soldiers and police. They would have their own radio communication, it seemed.

The moment of play lasted a short time before Hempel walked in and stood next to Alex. She crossed her arms as he again began to speak. "The forces of Order seek an artifact, and we cannot allow them to have it. We are unsure why it is so important to them, but it is. And they plan to steal it. Tonight. We plan to not let them."

******

Jamie landed upon the ground outside a large marble building. She knew from the briefing that she was outside a private museum amid the city sprawl of a dying suburb in a southern US city she had never heard of. As she had come to expect, she was the first to land, and it gave her a chance to scout the world around her. It was night here, and she could not but be partially thankful for the cover of darkness. Of course, it was a cover her enemies could use as well, if they were already here. She moved into the cover of a recessed window as the rest of her team started to land. Her vantage point gave her a good view of the surrounding area, and she continued to assess it, as she had been trained. She clicked her throat one time as the signal that all was clear before moving farther down the building.

The team came up behind her just as she reached a single blank door with a security light next to it and camera above. She felt safe behind the mask of the new uniform that Alex had provided her just for this type of mission. The suit was a dark maroon trimmed in black. It clung to her athletic body like a padded glove. It was tight enough to be a second skin, and the high neck opened to reveal her ruby collar. The mask matched her collar, and its gems shone in the moonlight. It was a red demon mask, and it covered her entire face. It had openings only at her mouth and eyes. Over it all, she had a thick, tailor-fit jacket with a deep hood that she had thrown up over her head.

She slammed into the door, passing through it in a spray of wood splinters and metal beams. She hit the ground and rolled up into a standing position. Nettle came in after her, and Jamie could not help but take a breath at Nettle in her new uniform. Unlike Jamie's fully covered form, Nettle's was less covered. She had her hair uncovered and tied back. A tightly woven scarf covered her lower face, so she looked like an outlaw cowboy in a cheap western. The scarf was pulled back around her head and tied in a large knot at the nape of her neck. The extra length hung down her back. Her shirt was open at the throat, showing off her obsidian collar. The shirt's neckline dipped low between her breasts. The amount of skin seemed to defeat the purpose of armor, and Jamie assumed she had to have taped it on to make it so formfitting and to keep it from falling off. Nettle's hands, arms, and legs were covered in a tight, thin material that looked like obsidian skin, it clung so tightly. Where Jamie's suit was padded, Nettle's looked like it was the same thickness as standard tights. A short skirt was wrapped around her waist in a strange bow to either modesty or style. The tights on her legs did little to cover how long and beautiful they were. Her boots laced up past her knees and reflected what little light existed in the hallway. The entire uniform was a solid blackness that shone in the night.

Jamie continued down the hallway, knowing that Nettle would follow her, and she hoped the others were getting into their positions. Another door loomed to block her path, and again, she took it in a tackling charge that left nothing to block Nettle's path. As Jamie slid to a halt, bent down on one knee, tight as a spring ready to uncoil, she saw that they were in a large room filled with a multitude of glass cases. She held her knives out in defense, and she quickly moved forward into the dark room.

The cases of glass held all manner of items. Jamie did not know or understand what made these items so important. Her quickly moving feet brought her through the room and to the entrance to the next. Nettle moved gracefully beside her, and they both peered into the room.

The middle of the room was empty, with cases and benches against the walls. A short-haired, blonde woman sat upon a bench across the room. She was clothed in dark green with golden highlights. Everything about what she wore screamed, "I just put this on five minutes ago, to answer the door in something, and not be naked." Her face was uncovered, and her bare hands were upon her knees. Jamie moved to the left of the room as Nettle stepped up in front of her, drawing the woman's eyes. Jamie knew how she must look, like a wraith guarding Nettle's beauty. A red demon shadow of the black statue approaching the blonde. Jamie felt powerful because of her own intimidating image. She let go of that pride and slunk further into the shadows, toward the wall.

"Dear me, look at you girls! So cute. A little red wagon and her charcoal spinning top. Tippy Tops are the funniest to spin. Are they here to steal what I must steal? Shall we see whose steel cuts whose steel?"

Nettle moved gracefully, until her outstretched sword was within feet of the blonde woman's face. Yet the woman never blinked her ocean-blue eyes, never took her eyes from Nettle's face. "Oh, oh, nice collar, little puppy top. Daddy give that to you?" The woman laughed and tilted her head to one side.

"Your Armies of Order will not stop us today."

The woman laughed a quiet, low laugh and stared Nettle in the eyes. "There are armies of Order and ordered armies, and yet none of them are my armies, little girl. I like the shinies and the pretties. Just here to pick up a little something-something and get on out. The Queen wanted me to try you on, wee child, but my wardrobe is much too flamboyant to fit in your closet."

With that confusing monologue, the blonde struck. She moved without moving. Jamie had no idea how to explain it. One minute, the woman was practically lounging on the bench, and the next, she was standing and moving, slipping up to stand facing Nettle's sword. She had not teleported. Jamie had seen every step, every move the woman had made from one point to the other. It had all just happened within a single smooth second. She appeared to be unarmed.

"You will not pass." The steel in Nettle's voice cut the air and stabbed the words into the blonde woman's ears.

But the woman just laughed again and placed two fingers on the cutting edge of Nettle's sword. "Will it be you who stops me, we think? We might not be sure." And again, the woman moved like the wind. She spun toward Nettle and into her cutting blade and past it, throwing out a hand that struck flesh and pushed Nettle two steps backward. Jamie looked up sharply from what she was doing with the case and took a step forward before remembering her place and stepping back again to the case. Nettle had made this plan. Nettle was her leader, and she had it well in hand. Nettle made a show of motioning Jamie back, as if to say, "This one is mine." Jamie backed to the doorway as Nettle charged into action.

The blonde was pushed back by the charge, but only temporarily, and the two women began a dance that was beautiful to watch. Nettle swiped high from the left, and the woman blocked the blow on her forearm. The sound of metal hitting metal filled the air. Nettle turned her graceful backswing into a full spin, coming full circle to cut low at the woman's back. The blonde flipped backward in the air over the blade. Head back, legs coming up and around, bringing her past the sword's path and to a landing with her feet upon the ground. She jabbed out with her hand aimed at Nettle's ribs, but as her hand struck, it had nothing but air and black lightning to pass through. Nettle rematerialized behind the woman and slammed the handle of her sword into the back of her head. The blonde bounced forward with a bone-jarring crunch. Nettle was quick, moving in to strike, but with a single shake of the head, the blonde was up and moving again with a turn towards Nettle. One outstretched hand grabbed Nettle's sword by the blade, holding it in place as the other hand flat-palmed Nettle in the chest, driving her into the air with a loud crash as she landed on her back and lay motionless.

Jamie sprinted for the door and was heading down the hallway when she heard Joe on the intercom, saying that they had company outside. From within the room, Jamie heard the blonde's frustrated cry as the woman must have realized that Jamie already held the odd gold disc and was running for the door that led outside. With a crack of black lightning, Nettle was running beside her, a smile of wild abandon on her face, a smile that Jamie hoped was a match for the one she felt on her own. The sounds of excessive violence followed them from the room they had left, as though the blonde was destroying everything in her reach.

Jamie and Nettle practically dove out into the night and across the street. They had entered through the back of the building, and they heard commotion at the front. A commotion they both veered toward without even talking. As they approached the corner of the building, Joe appeared next to the wall. His invisibility dropped, and he closed ranks with them as they sprinted around the corner. He wore a thick armor of solid white that covered him from head to toe. His mask looked like something from a science fiction novel or a kid's show, but then so did the whole outfit. It looked like long, thick ivory on his tall frame.

Standing at the top of a wide wooden staircase was Russ,

blocking the path through two massive double doors. He stood like a Viking warrior, pointing his large ax down at a crowd dressed in loose-fitting grey outfits at the base of the stairs. Russ' uniform was dark blue with light blue trim and a touch of gold threading here and there. His face was uncovered by a mask, but a thick covering of paint swirled and whirled across his face and arms. His arms were bare from the shoulders down, and a thick, pleated vest hugged his muscular frame. It was unbuttoned at the front, making it seem almost as low-cut as Nettle's shirt. Russ had obviously adjusted it to better show off his chest. The vest hung down over his pants to his thighs. His pants were almost like jeans, with the dark blue coloring and close-cut. They ended in a pair of large, thick boots that Russ stomped as he spoke to the crowd of warriors at his feet. He most definitely filled the space with his personality, and the sound of his argument reached even Jamie's ears despite the roughly two hundred yards between them. She picked up the pace and felt herself pulling away from Joe and Nettle, who raced behind her.

Whatever conversation Russ had been having seemed to break down as he waded from the stairs into the crowd below, his ax now doing all the communicating. From behind where he had stood, María now stepped up, with the most imperious look a person could have. The crowd beneath her was well beneath her, that look said. She cupped a golden ball of light in her outstretched hand, and the flames of gold that flicked out of it brought screams to those below her. Her uniform was more like Jamie's in shape, because it had pants and a long-sleeved top of a thick material woven tightly around her body. But it differed in its elegant style. Her shoes looked like comfortable runners, rather than the knee-high boots that Nettle had favored. The entire outfit seemed to be made of a golden chainmail that glinted in the lights from the building and moved like a dragon's scales as María turned and threw the golden globe she held into the crowd, where it exploded like a grenade. The multitude of small, overlapping scales was breathtaking. María's uniform had no hood, and her mask was a simple veil made from thin golden mesh that hung lightly over her face before weaving up into her hair. The veil hung to her nose, leaving her red lips open to the night. The many unwoven strands coming off the veil filled her hair with a thousand golden strings to highlight the raven darkness of her long locks. She seemed to sparkle each time she threw a bolt of light at the crowd. She was the shiniest object the world had ever seen.

Jamie had, by now, closed to roughly one hundred yards and cleared the remaining distance in moments. The crowd was so focused on Russ and what looked like Carlisle clashing that they did not feel the threat at their backs until Jamie had already cut down three of them. She was a spinning dervish of death amongst them. The grey-clad crowd's reactions were slowed by shock as her own were just cycling up to cut into them. She could not see, but she sensed Nettle cut down a woman to her left before spinning off into the rest of the crowd, creating space between them to work.

It was a bloodbath as they danced, and it was over as quickly as it had started. By the time the crowd of warriors broke and ran, they had been decimated by the Chosen among them. Only Carlisle remained to stand against them, and even his quick parries and inhuman strikes had slowed to an almost manageable pace, now that all five of the Chosen were involved and working in unison to strike at him. He made no noise as he struck and retreated, over and over. Judging by the speed at which he moved, Jamie still felt that their combined might was likely insufficient to best him.

Jamie charged in, knives low, but just as she should have cut into Carlisle's thigh, the handle of his sword connected with her face, driving her into the pavement. He swung down in a mighty arc that would have connected with her head had Russ' ax not been there to block it. Carlisle's backswing would have taken Russ' head if a string of golden missiles had not forced him first to block then step back to where Nettle's sword swung at him. He had no choice but to block her strike first to the left, then Joe's staff to the right, moving back and forth between them. The bright flash of Joe blinding his opponent filled the night. Jamie flipped from her prone position to fully standing and dove in, slamming into Carlisle's stomach and knocking them both to the ground. Jamie rolled through the fall and came up on her feet. The charge had knocked Carlisle too far off balance, and he hit the ground hard on his side before pushing himself up and raising his sword over his head in preparation to attack. He looked winded. He squinted, which made Jamie think Joe had struck gold. An animal joy took Jamie, and she felt her body preparing to pounce.

And like that, Carlisle stepped back and was gone. Leaving Uazit's Chosen with their first victory and a pile of bodies. Jamie felt the adrenaline leaving her body as she sat on the steps and breathed. The fight had filled her with a joy greater than any in her life. The battle blood of ancient warriors ran through her veins and pumped joy at a fight well-fought. Her teammates looked equally fierce and beautiful. They had been made for this.

Russ looked at the ground at his feet. He was blood-soaked, and his large ax hung low, dripping. Jamie realized he was staring at the small pool the dripping from his ax had created. Nettle... Sweet, sweet Nettle stared off in the direction Carlisle had run as if debating whether to run after him. She was a racehorse waiting for the gate to drop and give her the signal to run. Looking at her leader, Jamie felt the answering call in her chest. If Nettle ran, Jamie would run with her.

María sat down next to Jamie and laid her head upon Jamie's shoulder with a contented sigh. She took Jamie's hand and just held it loosely as they both watched Russ and Nettle. Jamie had never felt so close to María. She could not help but feel that the other girl was the only one in the group who found as much joy in the fights as Jamie did herself. Jamie had seen the look in María's eyes in that first fight, when María had burned out the woman's eyes and mouth with power. She looked serene and beautiful in a way Jamie had wanted to hold. Her head on Jamie's shoulder was comfortable, and her hand was cool yet warm. It was a moment of contentment and connection.

Jamie patted her chest with her free hand and felt under her jacket the golden disc that they had come for. It called to her with power. It sang, and she knew it was special. It echoed her own power. All in all, a job well done, and a plan well made. The blonde woman had never joined the fight. In fact, once they had left the building, Jamie had not seen her anywhere. Perhaps she had been there as a thief only. It was one thing to steal for money, a completely different one to die for it. Either way, Jamie hoped to see her again. Something about the woman had put her in a good mood. As she contemplated all they had done, she noticed Joe staring at her with a worried look on his face. She tried to give him an encouraging smile, but he just turned and followed Nettle's gaze into the nothing. She laid her cheek against the top of María's head and quietly watched her teammates.

VISIONS OF DISTRUST

There are dreams of fire that fill us and burn away that which is impure. You know this. We all know this. The danger comes when the fire burns, and we have nothing pure to hold onto. When the fire that tests, is a test we must fail. What happens then? When we burn and burn, and we are not tested by the fire but destroyed. We must find our own way, become our own phoenix. We must spread our ashes upon the earth.

Jamie stood on a shore, watching wave after wave of thick salt water crash against the sand. She could taste it in the humid air—the salt and pain around her. It tasted clean and purifying in a way that choked her and made it hard to breathe. She gazed out over the ocean's edge, pounding against the ground. An unrelenting assault on the solid earth that dared rise above the water's ego. The sand washed away in that pounding and swirled in dirty jetties of copper-tasting colors, like blood washing from a hand.

The stars shone above her as the moon dipped behind her. She could see herself standing like a long-forgotten statue staring into the sea. Sorrow-filled eyes at the neglect the world had shown her. Her dark hair hung down her back and face in salty, wet curls and in gritty tracks of sand and grime upon her dark skin. She was some ancient African goddess erected upon the shore in a time when her tricks were still exalted. She stood pointing out to sea. Pointing to where those who dared upset her should be driven. Her naked skin a taste of coffee on the night. Her dark eyes peered into unknowable depths with a twinkle of mischief and malicious intent.

She was solitary and complete. She was an island unto herself as the waves continued their relentless rolling. Sprays of water geysered up around her with each hammering of sand by wave. The tides had come in, covering her feet in pools of wisdom while the water's spray hovered around her in a mist of ignorance. And yet she did not move. The wisdom wanted to rise up and drown her while the mist continued its choking hold upon the air.

The night sky was muddy, as the morning light rose upward from the watery depths of the horizon. She looked at it there before her, that line of light growing with each crash of the waves. Blue and gold stars twinkled in the blackness of the sky, but they were soon drowned out by the coming light. The dark hues of the world brightening, as change took what was into what would be. The stars and the darkness seemed like they were screaming as they drowned in that light. They struggled against the pure white light. Jamie choked for a moment on her feeling of loss as the one star outshone the others.

As happens in dreams, laughter built within her for no reason. She felt the wind of the night embrace her as it raced away from the sun. It begged her to follow it into the sky. The voices cried out to her.

"Do not stand and watch."

"Do not wait for the painful coming."

"Do not wait for the next moment."

"Flee the morning star, for today you cannot defeat it."

A deep sorrow filled her as the morning sun rose before her in a blinding whiteness that filled the earth with its horrifying life. The kisses of darkness slipped up into the heavens, a distant memory of the night. Jamie had waited too long to act, and now, the day betrayed the night.

The pain began as soon as the morning light kissed her

face. She could feel it burning like a soft caress upon her skin. Painful points of soft lips tracing every inch. The white light intensifying and scorching deep into her being. This mouth was not kissing her with the soft lips of a lover but devouring her with the sharp ripping teeth of a killer. The love she thought had lived within the light was a thin covering for the hatred that lived in its flaming depths. Her body began to smoke and smolder before catching fire. In a deep white light of betrayal, she felt her being burn away into ash. The ash floated up and away upon the ocean wind.

She became the wind, the particles floating like pollen into the world, giving her own life to the seeds she touched and spreading a crimson blanket of flowers and fruits in her wake. This was her legacy, to burn away all that she was to finally give wild beauty to the world. Generations from now, they would redden their lips on the sweet taste of her berries and adorn their hair with the wild flowers of her life. She was contented then, contented to grow her garden of crimson light.

Jamie woke to the comfort of her own contentment. Her bed cupped her body like a protective father's arms. The feeling of contentment still floated around in her mind, uncaught by the hooks of reality that eventually drag all dreams to their deaths. Her bed was warm, and she dreaded having to climb out from under the blankets to greet the day. But she knew she eventually must. She put it off by remembering the night before.

They had returned late, and she had barely had time to shower the blood from her skin before sleep took her in its warm embrace. She had wanted a leisurely shower of warm rain and instead had found the ocean in her dreams. The battle had gone well, and the disc had been retrieved. She smiled at that under her blankets. They had accomplished something, and proven their worth while doing it.

The golden disc had called to her power as she Traveled home. It had promised joys beyond her dreams and powers beyond her ken. It had sung there in her jacket, so close to her heart. The feel of it was warm and comforting, with deadly promise and tantalizing temptations. It promised to be hers, and only hers, if only she would answer its call, but it was a call she knew not how to answer.

Alex had smiled upon their return, and Hempel had debriefed them, pulling every bit of information she could about how the mission had gone. She seemed especially keen to learn about Carlisle. She warned them that he was much too dangerous to face at their stage, but she was still frustrated that nobody had killed him. They really should have killed him. She questioned them about the blonde (or The Blonde, as Nettle called her) and seemed interested in who the stranger might be.

Jamie knew that in the days ahead, Hempel would use their stories and retellings to break down what they had done and improve upon it for the next time. A sharp criticism would come, followed by hard training, but even this made Jamie smile. She would be better after pushing through the flame. Hempel would crush their egotistical rendition in order to ensure that their egos had hooks to hang upon.

Alex seemed especially proud that Nettle's plan had worked. A Trickster's plan, he called it. Two bright and shiny targets to distract at the door and pretend to be the assault. Two others in through the back door. One to confront any resistance and the other to retrieve the artifact under their noses. Bring it all together with their invisible lookout, and they were a regular "old sneaky-sneaky," as he liked to say.

Alex was especially interested in the disc, which he took and stared at for several moments in silence before studying each side and edge of it like a coin collector verifying the authenticity of Queen Elizabeth's personal penny. He hooted once and then turned a solemn eye on them and asked what the hell the thing was. Nobody had really known, so the kids were shooed off to bed, leaving the teachers to do whatever it was they did at night.

Jamie lay there in bed, remembering it all, still luxuriating in comfort, when Nettle and Joe barged into the room, unfairly fully dressed and chipper in the morning light. Nettle was tearing off strips of bacon with her mouth as she threw herself onto the bed next to Jamie, laughing. The soft thump of her body a sudden weight pulling Jamie towards her. A sudden insecurity gripped Jamie as she realized she had not dressed after her shower the night before. With the short skirt and tube tops Nettle favored, this left a lot of potential skin-to-skin contact, because only a thin sheet separated Jamie's nudity and the other girl's skimpy attire. Jamie glanced down at a long, beautiful leg lazily thrown over her own. She could feel the soft skin through the sheet as Nettle's leg slid slowly up her own. If Nettle noticed, she made no mention.

Joe was laughing and recounting his moves from the fight at the museum. His basketball shorts and t-shirt were baggy enough they flowed around his frame during his dance. His spirits seemed brighter than when they had left the bodies upon the field. A little sleep and reinterpretation of his actions seemed to have filled him with excitement about what he had done. He danced around Jamie's room with a glow upon his tan face. His smile was beautiful. The morning light did him justice, and Jamie could not help but smile at how much good the sunshine seemed to do him. This was not the same boy who had looked sadly upon the aftermath, but then Jamie knew that they all wore many masks.

"Get up, get up, get up." Nettle's words sprinkled around her head as the girl rolled this way and that, messing up the perfect nest Jamie had made. Her excitement was contagious, and the room glowed with Jamie's two friends. The two girls both laughed then lay back, limbs intertwined, watching as Joe continued his recital and sparred with the air. Jamie was filled with a joy at her friends that she could not express. She had people who cared for the real her and not the mask she wore. Her team had no expectations of her to weigh down their love. Something had broken loose within them all, after the museum and Vegas. They had found their purpose, the ceremony of their lives. They did not need their masks firmly attached, it seemed. What that meant she did not know, but right now, it meant she could laugh and mean it.

Nettle leaned over Jamie's body and stared into her face as if to share a secret joke, but at the last second, the other girl stopped, frozen, staring. The weight of her straddled Jamie's leg, fitting like a jigsaw puzzle. Their eyes met, and a flash of need filled Jamie. Nettle smiled, a deep smile. She reached out with her hand and touched Jamie's face. It was a soft, warm touch that drove an electric current through Jamie's skin and down her body. For a second, she remembered her dream and a furtive wind that had danced along her skin. The touch lasted a second only before Nettle crammed the last of her piece of bacon into Jamie's mouth and then threw herself in a haphazard, joyful roll off the bed and onto the floor. She grabbed Joe by the shirt and dragged him out of the room, singing aloud, "Up and at 'em." And then the hurricane of Jamie's friends was gone. Her cheek still burned with the feel of a warm hand, and her leg was covered in the weight and warmth of memory. She smiled and got up, enjoying the sweet, salty taste of bacon on her lips.

Breakfast was served, and as evidenced by Nettle's gift, it included bacon. Jamie dug in as the rest of the team finished. María smiled at her over a cup of the blackest coffee the world had ever seen. Her red lips gently caressed the golden mug's edge as they sucked in the dark liquid, creating a contrast in colors. Jamie could not help but feel a touch of envy and premonition, which she took to mean that she needed to pour her own mug.

Alex's coffee was always the best, and today's did not disappoint. It was thick and strong and filled her mouth with deliciousness. Jamie began a back-and-forth of bacon and toast, then coffee. She loved the salty followed by the bitter. But her food revelry was cut short when Alex held up the golden disc with a flourish.

"You have each had a night to think, so who knows what this thing is?" The silence echoed around him, and he sighed with obvious disappointment. "Well, I do not know, either. It has power about it. I can feel that. We will need to find out what it does and how we can use it. For now, what we do know. It is old, it is gold, and it has a picture of a lady stamped on one side but nothing on the other." He flipped the disc into the air and caught it like a gambler deciding where to eat breakfast. "Oh, and we know Order wishes to have it, so we keep it."

With that, he flipped it into the air one more time before catching it and slipping it into the pocket of the athletic shorts he wore, before leaning back in desolation against his chair, like every obstinate teen who had ever lived. He looked down at the table and rapped it a few times with his knuckles before looking back up. "Still, nobody... Well, then let us begin the lessons of the day."

And lessons they did while canoeing up the river next to the estate. Alex found topics upon topics to discuss and grill them about. The river was rough that day, and the clouds covered the sun. A coarse breeze battered the boats and threw sprays of water into the air. It pulled swirls through the water's eddies. The clouds darkened around noon, threatening rain upon all their heads. And within the hour, the sky had fulfilled its threat with a light rain. Jamie had found that the Coeur d'Alene area was beautiful, but the weather was fickle. A sunny day could turn to rain and drench a shirt before freezing the arms and ending in sunshine. Lightning could fill a clear sky, let alone a rainy one. Today seemed only to be getting worse. Still, Alex had them row on as if it was another sunny day.

He skirted the issue of the disc and discussion of it. The closest he came to the problem was to discuss the issue of problem-solving. "Throughout life, children, we are faced with problems we must solve. It is not a new issue. The question of how to solve problems has been around a long time. In ancient China, it was common for people to test wise men, to see just how wise they were. Their answers were often used to teach others how to live their lives. One such test was given to three sages, each man wise in his own path. They were revered and treated well by the king who brought them before him. They were asked to find the best way to cross a raging river.

"The first sage said that only through discipline and ordered movement could one safely cross the river. He believed that one should learn each rock on the riverbed and each current in the river. You could then use this knowledge to create a strict plan of how to cross. Think not only of the first step, but of every step you would take within the river. The dangers of the river could only be avoided by adhering to this rigid plan.

"The second sage said that one must take each step at a

time, weighing and measuring as one went. Test the waters and allow your body and mind to find the best path through the river's current at that moment. Think only of the first step. Only when it is completed and you know it is correct do you take the second step. Only by this testing and feeling of the water, one step at a time, could one really cross the river in safety.

"The third sage looked at the other men and shook his head. The best way to cross a river was to dive in and hope the rocks and rapids didn't kill you before the current carried you across.

"The question, of course, becomes not which man is correct, but when are they correct."

The gentle burbling of the water filled the empty space after his words as he quieted. The tender swoosh-swoosh of the paddles striking water pierced the silence. The incessant drops from the sky slapped softly against the river's surface like an echo of coins jangling in a pocket. Between a slight mist and the falling rain, the bank was a murky mirror image of itself.

Jamie had heard this called a "miserable wet," but to her, it was a moment to be alive. The fresh patter of rain on her face and arms cooling her body as she moved, one stroke after another. She laughed into the silence of herself and the rain. It was a release of tension and worry. It was a moment of expert wisdom that pulled her in and refused to let her go. She did not struggle against it; she just let it flow out of her like the river flowed beneath and the clouds flowed above.

Her entire body shook with her laughter, and she had to stop rowing. A deep, guttural laugh that shook her body and covered her mind like a veil. How long it lasted she did not know, only that it had taken as long as it had taken. She felt clean after it. A sense of deep-down purity and calm she had not felt in a long time. She was made to struggle, to find peace in the center of chaos. And this was, to her, a beautiful day.

When Jamie did stop laughing, the others were looking at her. Their paddling had ceased, and they looked bewildered. Russ and Joe looked worried at her outburst. They must have thought she had gone crazy to laugh on what, to them, must be a "miserable day." Nettle looked at her with quiet acceptance, like a parent coddling a spoiled child. She smiled, but it seemed more from dismissal than real happiness. Only María smiled as if she had joined in the laughter. She shook her head and tapped the side of Jamie's canoe with a playful knock before digging the oar into the water and pushing ahead of everyone. Jamie took chase of the now-laughing Mexican girl. The others behind them struggling to catch up, unsure if they wanted to.

By the time the lesson was over and they had returned

home, Jamie was soaked to the bone. The light patter had become a deluge that had filled her canoe and covered her in cold kisses. And they were kisses. The rain had started soft and gentle, with light pecks here and there, but mostly along her face. As it had grown in fervor, it had deepened to long, languishing caresses before engulfing her every inch. And she could feel it, the gentle touch along her arms and legs and face where the rain had ravished her.

María was still laughing with her, and they were splashing at each other as they pulled the boats onto shore. It was a happy feeling that Jamie connected with their win at the museum, a good night's sleep, and a feeling of acceptance she had never really had before. She looked at the others in their misery and could not help but share another secret smile with María before they ran toward home to dry off for dinner. The two girls playfully raced along the way in a childish game of tag.

The wet rats of the team trailed behind, all ineffectually scrunched over, trying to keep the rain and wind from digging through their clothing. Their posture only added to their look of desolation. They did not run, but they did not dawdle. Instead, they slunk back toward the dark, looming buildings. Their seemingly unbothered teacher watched everything and maintained a rueful smile as he meandered along at his own pace.

His slack step and jaunty attitude told the world that the rain made him no more sad or happy than a summer day would. He merely was what he was, and the world could not change him for better or worse. The wind passed through him.

After dinner, the trio of Jamie, Nettle, and Joe was walking the halls when Joe suddenly turned serious. "Do you trust Alex?" The question was unexpected. "I mean, he sent us after that disc without even knowing what it is." His voice made Alex's order sound ridiculous.

"He knew Carlisle wanted it." Nettle sounded defensive of their master, and Jamie was satisfied to let these two hash out the topic. They often discussed odd things, and Jamie just liked to listen to them—Joe with his fresh voice and Nettle's punctuated by drags on a cigarette.

"Right, right, but I mean... We risked our lives for something, and we don't even know what it does."

"We will. We just have to trust."

"Can we trust? Is that a thing we are capable of?" Joe's emphasis on "we" was pronounced and plaintive.

"I trust Alex after all these years, so yes, I think it is." Nettle's smoke-filled rebuttal seemed to deflate Joe, and he wandered ahead a little way before turning back.

"I trust you guys, so I guess you're right." Joe's smile said that all made sense again in the world. And they continued to walk the hallways with safer subjects they could all agree on. At some point, Joe disappeared behind the doors of his own room, with the excuse that he had some reading to do. This left Nettle and Jamie to wander alone.

"Did you notice Russ and María never walk into a room together?" Nettle's question threw Jamie off as they stopped and turned to each other. She replayed the sentence in her mind as she tried to make sense of it. There was a hint of jealousy and desire in the tone, but Jamie might have imagined it. Russ and María were always standoffish, in a silly kind of way. But they often joked, and Jamie had seen them take walks together. María's red lips filled her mind for a moment.

"No, but it makes sense, I guess. They always argue."

"Sense it makes, yes." Nettle winked and took a drag.

"You don't mean... You think?"

"Look, all I am saying is that if groups of humans always do the same thing over and over, it is because of a plan. And plans are often to hide the truth."

With that, they walked in companionable silence until they reached Jamie's door, where Nettle stopped and took her hand.

"Dream well and awaken. I'll see you in the morning."

"What does that mean—awaken?"

"Oh, just something Alex has always said since I was a kid. One of his many phrases he likes to reuse from the old days, I imagine." And with that, Nettle was off down the hall, leaving Jamie staring at her door.

She was curious what Nettle had meant about Alex and his reuse of phrases. She had never seen the man reuse anything. Not even shoes. He seemed in a state of constant change. But Nettle seemed to know more about him than anyone else did. Jamie wondered how that must be, to know him well enough to have seen him reuse things and to get to know his idiosyncrasies well enough to adopt them. Her mind's eye turned the gears of thought as she let herself into her room.

Jamie took a long, hot shower that comforted her and cleared her mind. She could not help but think about what Nettle had said about María and Russ, though. Did Jamie mind? She did not think so. She tried to imagine them together, and the image did not seem to want to form. Instead, she kept imaging Nettle in the place of Russ. Nettle taking María against a wall. Nettle looking down at María with a look of satisfaction. The warrior and the princess woven into one.

Jamie found she needed to change her thoughts, in the interest of comfort. Nettle had also talked about Alex. She knew him so well. How long had she been his student? What had happened between them, for her to know him so well? These thoughts kept breaking into Jamie's happier fantasies. A distraction from her mind's distractions.

Jamie had changed into a loose top and sweat pants for bed but had not yet crawled in when Alex walked through her door. She could not help but wonder if he had heard her thinking about him and had come to berate her into keeping her thoughts to herself. He had not visited her room since he had given her the necklace.

He did not knock. Jamie was not sure she had heard him knock on a door since he had first knocked at her apartment. The man had called the estate his own, and he seemed to mean all of the estate. So no, she could not expect a knock. He seemed oblivious to the entire idea of knocking. If there was a door open, you walked through; closed, you opened it. He only cared about his destination.

Alex had changed clothes at some point—into loafers, tan khakis, and a light green polo. He looked like a businessman trying to look informal but not really sure how to pull it off. Jamie imagined him standing at a coffee machine or water cooler, discussing a weekend of golf. She shook her head and wondered if there was a purpose to how he dressed. If Nettle were here, would she know why he had chosen this particular mask for whatever they were going to talk about?

If there was a reason for Alex's attire, he was not about to explain it. He sat himself upon Jamie's couch and moved his legs into a lotus position, staring at her. He should have looked ridiculous in loafers but he did not. If he was unnerved or uncomfortable about being in a pajama-dressed young lady's room unsupervised at night, he did not show it. He was just joining an old friend for an old chat. Like knocking on doors, he did not seem affected by most social pressures. They just did not occur to him unless they were part of his act of the moment. He sat comfortably in his position and smiled. The golfing monk, she thought, and giggled.

"When I tried to teach all of you to Listen, everyone failed, but your failure was the most spectacular."

His words were like a bomb dropped on her. She had tried as hard as she could; she always did and was proud of her ability with the power. She opened her mouth to defend her attempt, and he waved his hand to silence her.

"Your failure was the most spectacular, because when you should have Listened, I saw that you had, instead, Seen." He smiled and waited for her to process. He often lapsed into uncomfortably long silences after pronouncements had been made, either by himself or others. Jamie used the time to register what he was saying. Once again, Jamie heard the capital letter. What did he mean—"Seen?"

Jamie sat up on her bed and mimicked Alex's lotus posture and opened her mouth to speak. Again, he waved his hand to silence her. His quiet eyes gazed into hers, and then they roamed all over her like a man buying a car. He took his time, and Jamie began to itch in the silence. She wanted to ask him what he meant, but something about him kept her quiet. He looked back up into her eyes, and seconds began to tick into minutes. "Did you wonder how I knew where to find you? Or were you curious about how I knew about the disc? Are you imaginative enough to wonder?" He seemed genuinely curious and yet completely uninterested in her response. "I was informed. I am informed of many things. Uazit informs me. The world informs me." Again, with his silent staring. Watching for her to chew upon and finally digest his words. He was a patient man in this, his eyes a relaxed mask of seriousness. Just as she had formed a question, he spoke.

"To See is an art. It is a coloring of the world through your lens. Uazit speaks to us all. But those that See do not only Listen to her words. They See. You have had dreams that hurt. They will come more frequently as you grow stronger. There will be waking dreams. Uazit will speak to you and show you what must be done. You will Listen and you will See." His eyes were pools of sorrow for her even as his mouth smiled.

Alex motioned her to sit up straighter and look deep into his eyes. There were flames there, dancing in the night. Flames of jade and green that wavered and danced around his pupils and intertwined with his irises. They were mesmerizing, and within them, Jamie saw living stars floating upon the sky and waves crashing upon a shore. She was drawn into those eyes, and her mind relaxed until there was nothing but the fire dancing and eating away at her. Her mind darkened and danced with the flame. It opened to a world beyond this world, and bathed in the cosmic light, she found Sight.

There were laughing children and dour elders moving through her mind. Bees buzzed through the wild jungles as a bird chirped in the distance. She saw an infant girl sucked up into a spinning eye of red, burning chaos as the infant floated upon a boat of jade. A large raven pecked at the hearts of his own family, his own murder while the night cried down upon him and his sister gnashed her teeth. A drunken old man with a turquoise staff kicked a long line of pipe that had crawled across the landscape like a black snake. A beautiful woman with not one but nine tails dancing behind her swam naked in the shadows, wearing only a golden mask. These sights filled Jamie in a stream of images, yet there was only one sight, one image, and that was the fire burning before her eyes.

The morning sun struck her window, pushing her from her reverie. The bright light hurt her eyes, and her hand came up to shadow them. Her room was quiet and empty. Alex was gone, as if he had never been there. She sat stiff in her lotus position, staring out her own window as the sunrise began her day. She wondered what she was being Shown. She resettled herself into the lotus position and prepared to spend the day learning.

DREAMS OF SEEING

The ice was cold and unforgiving. She lay crying upon the barren wasteland, in a world of stark whiteness. The land pushed hard against her in sharp edges that cut into her bare back. The shock of cold was a dull ache as her breathy cries froze in the air around her face. The moisture was sucked from her wet skin, and it hardened into an icy shell. Her infant's body cried again, but her infant's mind realized it was too late to cry. She quieted and looked up at the bright, white sky above her.

If she had been older, she might have wondered why life was so unfair, taking her so young. Still an infant and left on the ice to die like a forgotten man tied and left in a ditch. She would have rued her fate and beaten upon the ground in silent, miserable victimhood. But she was not older. She was fresh-born, and this was the only world she had ever known. This harsh, unforgiving landscape was the first sight she had seen. The initial burning shock of cold was the closest she had ever come to understanding that things had once been different.

She did not know anything but this struggle to survive. In her few short moments of life, she had already begun to process how close she was to death. Cries only served to waste heat. The closest she came to realizing the unfairness of it all was to wonder why she would be born with this naked, sensitive flesh, so feeble against the onslaught of the world. But this was the only skin she had ever known, and it had always burned with cold.

There was a slight protection as the blood and wet of her birth froze upon her skin. It created a slight, if delicate, shell that trapped in a minuscule amount of heat. But even that minuscule amount mattered in such extremes, where frost was the only protection a naked infant could hope for.

She should not have survived the first moments on the subfreezing ice. She should not have survived her first breaths in this world. But she did, and she followed those breaths with more. Her first enemy was the world around her. Her first struggle was to breathe. Her first battle was to survive. Her first war was to live. And live she did, naked and alone in a small, mewling frame. For how long she lay, she did not know. But eventually, her understanding of the world was interrupted.

A dark blue-black shadow blotted out the sun when it bent

over her. The dark, hard beak that filled her small hands breathed warm breath upon her frozen skin. She could feel the sharp claws encircle her small frame, lifting her off the ice and into the sky. The wind beat against her in long, warm strokes of wings reaching for the sky. She was pulled up and embraced by the blue-black night. It felt like heaven.

Jamie rolled in her sleep, the sound of wings beating in her ears. The cold still clung to her skin. It was a comforting embrace as she rolled onto her back.

It was night as she ran, hunched over under the stars. She ran with the joy that such freedoms always bring. The fields in the world were open and ready. She felt intoxicated yet steady. The dirt gave beneath her feet as she charged over it. A line of darkness was crawling across the land before her. Crawling from horizon to horizon. The earth twisted under her and threw her up into the air.

The black line turned, and as it rose, it became a gigantic, dark snake. The scales were black and greasy as they shone under the stars. It was at once beautiful and ugly, in her sight. Fangs struck at her, and she dodged to the left and past the snake's head. She clambered upon its greasy, oily body and struck it with her fists. A musty, musky smell bit down on Jamie's tongue and nostrils, and she felt the urge to spit. She struck again and felt the scaly flesh give. Black blood stung her hand like acid. The snake bucked, and she flew backward into the air.

She struck the ground with an oomph and clouds of dust. The thick cloud of dust filled the field and then the sky. It was a brown, gritty mist that floated in the air before her and made it hard to breathe. She rolled onto her stomach and crawled along the ground, trying to spot the snake. Her only chance was to get close to it before it could spot her.

As she crawled, she heard a distant yip in the air that was echoed again and again around her. She felt her reply building in her throat, but it never came. Instead, the dark, thick diamond of the snake's head struck from the dust storm with long, thick fangs.

With a cry, Jamie leaped toward the striking serpent, grabbing it by the fangs and forcing its mouth apart. She had long metallic arms. The snake reared back, but Jamie held strong, knowing that if she let go, those venom-dripping teeth would sink into her flesh. She pushed back, bending the neck and head over the body. The snake moved in a flash of muscle and scale, flipping along the ground like a cracking whip and wrapping itself around Jamie's body in long, thick, ropy lengths. She could see no way out. Her hands gripped the bright and shining fangs as the dark, greasy scales of its body wrapped around her body and began to constrict.

Her world turned black and was covered in oily darkness.
She struggled but knew her world was already fading away.

She could feel her blankets wrapped around her, and she
threw them off. Jamie felt the soft sounds of her room as her
body slipped to its side and curled in around itself.

She stood like a shadow in the dark church. The building
was old and crumbling. The walls curved up around her into the
darkness above. Candlelight twinkled here and there along the
walls, in brief bright sections of illumination, leaving the majority
of the empty room dark. As in many dreams before it, the
darkness and light seemed unnaturally more than they could ever
be in life. A short, dark woman danced at the front of the room.
She was the most beautiful woman Jamie had ever seen.

She wore a gown of many ivory and gold veils, hanging
loose upon her body and moving with a translucent grace around
her. Her dance seemed to be an eclectic mix of movements that
bled together in a single strand. She undulated like a belly dancer
before moving quickly in turns and pirouettes. The white and
gold veils danced along her body, and as they moved, they
revealed splashes of multicolored veils underneath. The thin,
transparent layers gave the impression that one could see the
outline of her full, curvaceous figure underneath. Her skin was

the color of coffee filled with cream. Her hair was a light brown and hung well past her knees in long, straight strands. It fanned out around her as she spun.

Her hands glinted in the light like long burning stars, reaching out. It took a moment for Jamie to realize the stars were long silver daggers. They sparkled in her hands as she turned and performed a flip. Jamie could see her perfectly shaped bare feet and tan legs as she glided around and landed smoothly into a pirouette. She threw her arms out around her and glided to the side. Her dance was a violent loveliness that would have torn any partner to shreds with her sharp blades. It was an exquisite yet savage beauty.

Beyond just the dance, the woman was stunning and had an aura of joy around her. As happens in dreams, the joy was a thick, cloying cloud that followed the woman around. It tinted the air like a physical entity. It was not the woman's joy but the joy of anyone who happened to enter the cloud. It sparkled in murky mirth around her. Jamie felt the pull to step closer. To enter that joy. To feel it. The temptation was stronger than she could resist, and she felt her body move of its own accord.

A rough, gripping hand pulled her back and threw her into the wall. Like the shadow that she was, she did not hit the wall but passed through it untouched. The eyes of an ivory mask followed her. Long, lithe fingers pointed the way. Jamie flew back farther and faster into darkness, and the mask flew after her.

She was standing in a flowering orchard under the night sky. The crisp, white flowers hung gently from the trees in the moonlight. They added to the glow around her. Shadows cupped an ivory mask like one would find at a carnival masquerade. The scent of fruit blossoms filled the orchard, and Jamie breathed deep, letting the sweetness fill her.

The mask rose, revealing a golden female form. The woman who stood before Jamie was tall and lithe, and every inch of her was gold. She did not seem to be wearing a golden suit, but rather had skin of solid gold. The ivory mask she wore shone brightly in the moonlight. Long, pale white hair drifted around her as if she floated in water. She was the living embodiment of the golden bowers topped in white flowers around them.

Her head tilted to one side as she regarded Jamie. Her long, nimble body seemed to untwist, and nine golden tails fanned out behind her. The fur on the tails looked soft and luxuriant, and Jamie immediately wanted to know what the tails would feel like wrapped around her. The woman floated over so that Jamie was looking up into the ivory mask. She could taste the scent of fruit flowers, and the scent grew as though it clung to the woman.

"You should not be seen by the Queen." The woman's voice was solemn. It was smooth and comforting, yet direct. Jamie felt the command.

"Who was that woman in the church? Who are you? What are all these dreams?" Jamie's words and questions flowed out of her in a rush. She was like a tethered balloon that had finally been released.

"You are Seeing." Again, with the hint of solemn command. The mask twisted this way and that, like the face of a bird attempting to get a better view. It leaned in and sniffed deeply along Jamie's body before a long tongue slipped out and licked her from neck to forehead. "You are Uazit's or...? No... no. I am right. I taste the Great Mother upon you. But His scent does cling as well." It sniffed again and then floated back, head twisted to the side.

They began to walk through the orchard—Jamie, with her long stride, and the ivory mask and golden body floating beside her. Its thick tails and white hair brushed against her with gentle tickles. The smell of flowers and grass wrapped around them with the wild abandon of natural life.

"Tell me, daughter of Spider, why do you travel my lady's land of dreams and spy upon our enemy the Queen?"

"I don't know. I don't know how I am here. I just dream."

"Yes, you have been 'just dreaming' in our realm a lot recently."

"Your realm—what is this place?"

"'This place,' as you call it, is the eternal Now. The bitter, broken futures of what may be and the sweet, salty pasts of what might have been are the happy multitudes that could be this moment if the past or future had played a different tune. You can learn to hear those tunes and play them. Here is where it all can be seen and felt. Known and taught. Today, you learned what it was to be Chosen by the other Tricksters. You were embraced by them all."

"Here, with you, how can I learn...," Jamie spun around, arms out, "this... all of this?"

"Come to me at times in the shadows, and we will learn. Come to me in the moment between moments, and we will teach."

Jamie considered the ivory mask as a golden hand rested upon her shoulder and thick golden tails and white strands wrapped around her form. As though an alarm were going off in her head, she knew she had to go. The shock of the images that flooded into her was a sharp and striking pain. She knew he was without his power. His face was covered in blood. She knew she needed to save him. She had to tell the team. She had to share her dream. This was her vision calling to her, commanding her to go and save him.

Jamie's body screamed as blackness overtook her and dragged her from the soft orchard's light. And as she drained down into her comfortably sleeping body, she heard the golden voice whisper behind her, "Ah, now I see whose child you truly are."

ADULTS SPEAK

Jenny's was a dive bar, by the look of it. Walking in, Carlisle was surrounded by a host of common dive bar staples. The wood-smoked paneling covered in old pictures and odd paintings. The old beaten copper bar that took up the whole left side of the long, narrow establishment. An old, hard-used yet well-cared-for pool table that sat at the back of the room. A mix-and-match of tables and chairs that took up the front area, begrudging room only to the old jukebox that sat against the wall like a beat-up contraption from a bygone area. The entire place screamed dive bar on the surface. But like most things in life, the surface was only there for those too lazy to look deeper, Carlisle had learned.

It only became apparent that the bar was anything but a true dive bar when Carlisle looked at the colorful bottles of high-end liquor that sat upon the shelves behind the bar. They glowed in the neon lights of the many signs hanging around them. The inventory was a mix of top-shelf booze and craft beers, with an asking price that the normal dive bar patron could never afford. The lack of visible price tags anywhere implied a clientele that never asked the cost of the things they wanted. This was a bar of class and wealth masquerading as a crappy little shithole.

The one employee was a medium-height Asian woman who seemed to be in her late thirties or early forties, leaning against the back counter. Her jeans and t-shirt screamed hipster youth, yet they rested on her frame like she had been working hard all day. She seemed to have been a natural beauty in her youth, and age had merely matured her beauty without denting it. Her youthful clothing and carefree stance only highlighted her classic features. Carlisle could see writing on her shirt but was unable to read it past her crossed arms. He assumed that in this setting, her shirt likely had some pithy remark subtly emblazoned across her chest. A different man on a different mission may have asked for her number over his first drink. Of course, the look on her face said that a different man would have been shot down.

There were currently no other guests beside the blond man sitting at the bar with a bowl and glass in front of him. His long hair was pulled back into a ponytail, and his athletic frame was wrapped in a navy blue suit that almost sparkled all the way down to the black cowboy boots he had up on the stool's legs. His look was of relaxed elegance enjoying the weekend. There was an aura about him of a man with his own soundtrack playing in his head. A soundtrack only he could hear.

The man could not help but have noticed Carlisle and his companions entering. And yet he never took his eyes off the dark beer and ancient chipped bowl in front of him. His attention was on his meal, and his spoon would dip and rise, not making a single sound throughout its journey. He sipped slowly from his spoon, and the shiny platinum watch on his wrist glinted in the light as he dipped his spoon for more. Carlisle walked over behind the man while his companions spread out around the bar. He had brought more companions than he thought he needed, but this was one opponent he did not want to underestimate. As the companions spread around the bar, Carlisle continued to close the distance between himself and the man he wanted to talk to. The only change was the man setting down his spoon and picking up his beer.

Carlisle stood there quietly, taking in the understated quality of the man before him. Carlisle tapped his sheathed sword against his thigh as he studied the man. Giving his companions more time to fan out throughout the bar, taking up positions to ensure they had every available position covered.

The man seemed relaxed, yet an aura of waiting energy seemed to surround him, like a high-tension power wire waiting to be touched to fill the world with sparks and power. The feeling that a wild animal waited under that suit permeated the very air around him. His suit was less glamorous than Carlisle's, yet Carlisle could see that the hand-stitching was of a better quality. At this distance, he could easily see the jade collar around the man's throat. A thing that should have been out of place against the neck of his suit, yet it seemed to fit perfectly with the long tie of blue and black that butted up against it.

Carlisle felt an instant connection with this man. He had never met him, yet he had been playing a game with him for some time now. Carlisle had heard of him. Of course, everyone had heard of him. He was a legend among people like Carlisle, a myth that until recently Carlisle had no more believed in than Superman. And here Carlisle was, matching wits against him. It was an honor and a risk. Carlisle was filled with sudden courage, knowing what he knew was about to happen. This was to be the greatest moment of his life, the greatest triumph.

The employee behind the counter looked at Carlisle as if waiting for him to order, but instead, Carlisle addressed the man before him. He strived to keep his voice steady and firm. Nothing would interfere with his enjoyment of this event. When his fighters bragged about it later, they would remember his power.

"I have a spoon." The man's words were a whispered laugh under his breath. For a minute, Carlisle was taken back at the seemingly childlike glee in the sentence.

"You know who I am, Alcibiades?"

"I do." Quiet. Composed. Unexpectant. The reply of a man stating a fact he cared very little about.

"You know why I am here?"

"I know you should not have come, but you have. Sit. Try the chowder. It is blend of salmon and halibut, with a delicious hint of spice, and truly goes good with the Wendigo Brown Ale. Jenny makes it all from scratch right back there in the kitchen. Well, except the ale. It comes from a local place down the road. Sit, we can talk. Enjoy a good meal. And afterward discuss moving on with why you are here. There are not enough times to enjoy a good meal with good honest conversation."

The employee moved toward the back of the establishment and disappeared behind an open door that it was easy to assume was the kitchen. Carlisle started to speak, and the man turned. His blue eyes burned bright and seemed to spear into Carlisle's very being. He was frozen in that gaze. The man's hard features drilled through him. Taking in all Carlisle was and had ever been. Carlisle would have been unsurprised if the man could recite every thought Carlisle had ever had just from that one moment. He felt violated and yet understood in ways he did not even realize were possible, and all from a burning look. From eyes that did not seem to really care.

Without understanding the feeling within him, Carlisle took a step back and held the sword still sheathed between them. His hands involuntarily began unsheathing his sword. He heard the movement of his people behind him. He had brought enough to fill the bar. A bee's nest of activity began to explode into the world, yet the man sat quietly, looking at Carlisle.

Carlisle had heard that some people had the look of a wild animal hiding behind their eyes. Shit, he had used a similar metaphor earlier to describe the man hiding the animal within the suit. But there was no hiding here. The wild animal was out and staring at him. Waiting for him to move wrong and be torn apart.

Was this fear he felt? Was it awe? Carlisle had been chosen to be who he was because he lacked the emotional spectrum of normal humans. It was what made him special. What made them all special. They were all free of such petty weaknesses. And yet, a shock of adrenalin filled his system—the understanding that he was prey. The understanding of why this man was a legend. Whatever the feeling was, it passed quickly.

Carlisle gathered himself and stepped toward the man, who had turned back to his drink.

Without thinking, Carlisle took the empty stool next to the man. And the buzz of activity stilled behind him. Before he could speak, let alone order, the employee placed a bowl of thick, creamy liquid before him and a dark beer next to it. He relaxed into the stool and set his sword on the bar next to his own chipped white bowl and picked up the old spoon. It really was very good chowder.

"Thank ya, ma'am. I am sure my friend will enjoy it."

The two men sat quietly and ate their stew. One silently, one with a steady slurping and sounds of enjoyment. They ate and drank in companionable comfort.

"The great Alcibiades. You know, your book changed my life. It changed all of our lives."

"That book." A head nod followed by a sip of beer. "I barely remember it. The past is so clear. So many memories. But parts of it are unimportant. Why remember it? I did not even know it was out there anymore to be found and read."

"Kay and I have spoken of it. What it means. We have spoken of many things. Discussed all the things that make the world better. Such as the collars the Chosen wear."

Alcibiades became almost motionless at the mention of Kay, and full stillness took him at the word "collars." Carlisle reached over and tapped the jade collar. "You see, she shared the power the collars give their wearers—that Uazit collars her Chosen while the other Gods give weapons and armor, tools and implements. But the collars make the wearer her weapon. Her tool. Her implement. What a fascinating secret, and for some silly thief to know it. To know that the great warriors of Uazit are just pumped up on their goddess' power. Weak without it." Carlisle could hear the laughter in his own voice, the smug satisfaction of showing off to a person he had revered for years. Meeting a celebrity and showing them his greatest trick. He felt smug. He felt powerful in this very moment. He could feel the greatness within him as he revealed his trick. What he had come here for.

"You see, she told me more than what the collar does. She told me how to remove it." With that, he tapped again upon the collar. This time with a flourish. The click was a rattle deep in the quiet bar, and deeper still in the world. It sang lower-pitched than Carlisle had ever heard anything sing before. This time with a flourish the collar came off with a click. The rattle was followed, for a moment, by the world's silence, as Carlisle set the collar on top of the sword. His body shook slightly, with his joy.

"You are the test, my friend. We get old boy alone. Mr. Washed-Up. Make sure it works. Then we get the kids." Carlisle could barely contain his ecstasy at this first and important step: the de-powering of the great man. Even if the days of Alcibiades' fighting were long over, the removal of his collar still meant that a figure of power had been knocked from the table. And Carlisle had been the one to do it.

The silent stillness of Alcibiades was trophy enough. But the man had to ruin the moment by talking in his smooth, easy tone about nothing. "Aw, Kay. It has been so long since I have seen her—my girl. Another memory shadowed by the now." Alcibiades waved the employee over. She gathered the bowls and glasses and carried them away to the back room. Alex pulled his spoon from his bowl before she took it. He made a production of sucking it clean before he set it on the counter in front of him. "I have much to thank her for. I will look back at what was and remember how to do that. Before I thank her, though, I shall have to thank you. A deep gratitude that will come thrice. But let's swing back to that. First, let's talk about your mistake." As the employee stepped back through the door, he waved her over.

"May I, dear girl, have the mix, please? Then, I think it might be time for you to take off. I will lock up before I go. Don't you worry, dear. All will be cared for." And as he spoke, he set three large bundles of bills on the counter and placed his finger on top of them, smiling at the woman behind the counter. He slid the bundles over the bar toward her. She pulled from under the counter a square tray with several bottles and fruit and glasses upon it. She set it in front of Alcibiades. She picked up the money and left through the kitchen.

"I have lived a long life. Too many memories to worry about. But you made a mistake. You threatened my kids. Those are mine." The venom of the last word shook the bar. For a long moment, Carlisle wondered at the control needed to hold in such anger. He had experienced his share of rage before, but this was enough venom that he heard swords drawn and guns pulled from the companions he had brought with him. The room felt jumpy, and the energy in it felt prepped, suddenly, for violence.

"Have you had the perfect old fashioned?" The phrase was a simple, easy question, as if all the poison that had filled him had never been. The entire room felt calm again, hollow. The tension Carlisle had felt a minute before was gone now. The entire room's energy drained away in a second by a single phrase from a single man. Alcibiades pulled two whisky glasses toward himself, allowing drops from two small bottles to drip into each glass. He followed this with cherries and a small spoonful of dark sugar. After gently using his spoon as a muddler, the glasses contained a mash of fruit and liquid. He then cut an orange that bled red instead of orange.

"You see, it is a perfect drink. You need the right bitters, obviously. Jenny has a nice stock. Same with her sugar, which I helped her search the world for. The perfect muscovado. The perfect sweetness. She, of course, allows me to make my own soaked cherries. Which takes months and a painfully exact mix of gin, cocoa nibs, and orange liquor. All of this muddled gently before adding a frozen whisky stone. And then, right in with the blood orange wheel. I was unhappy with the oranges around here, so years ago, I planted several trees I liked around. You really must ensure that the ingredients you need are around in both quantity and the highest quality." Alcibiades slowly mixed it all together, and from an icebox he pulled a whisky stone to drop into each glass. On top of the stones, he placed a thin slice of blood orange.

"Finally, a gentle pour of the best bourbon or rye whisky you can find. Here, we are using an ancient bourbon. Never again to grace the world. The last two glasses of the entire batch. But, you know, it being your last drink, I thought you might like it. The hint of caramel really comes through. Divinity. Have a drink here. Please, a gentle drink, if you will. Taste that. That encompasses everything that came before it and washes it all away. So much work. So much time. So much need. And yet, the truth is—all of that, for what? What you are really adding are a few subtle undercurrents in the whisky that is already there." Alcibiades sipped the drink with a sigh of relief. The look on his face spelled paradise. Carlisle took a sip and realized only then that this was, in fact, a drink to pray for.

"Yet it is the greatest drink you will ever taste. Do you feel that immediate warmth? That delicious touch of fog that helps you to enjoy everything that will come later? Now you see what I mean. The memory of the soup that came before is of so little importance, you barely remember it. It was so on the tip of your tongue only moments ago. It is in the past now. The past you no longer require. Because now, now is the time for a nice, fine drink. All of this before I say thank you." Carlisle gently sipped from his glass. He watched Alcibiades do the same. The drink hit him with a hot burn that really did wash away everything else. A feeling of completion that spread down his throat and into his guts. The man did seem to know his food and drink. Carlisle thought, no reason not to let the man have his last drink.

A few sips in, Alcibiades turned to Carlisle. "You speak of Kay, my sweet Kay, whom I have missed with an ache in my heart. My greatest memories are showing her the world that should now be hers. Tell me, Man of Order, how is Griselda, my dearest

Queen. Is she happy?"

The sound of her name filled the room with joy, yet Carlisle almost sputtered out his drink to hear it grace this man's lips. "You know of Griselda?"

The man's laugh was rich and full and almost human. The humor of it felt real and rich. "The world knows the Queen. As for her name, I should think I would know my wife's name quite well. Now, is she happy?"

"But... I had heard... I had heard Uazit...?"

"Oh, yes. I met Uazit after already having been married for longer than most people live. Back then, no one blinked an eye at more than a single spouse. Not many people know who are and who are not my spouses. The happiness we all once shared on those warm ocean voyages together. Back then, we all lived together in joy. The world was ours to taste. I love them both. They have made a mess of our world, I suppose. Griselda was my first love. We were so young. She is a memory that will never stop being important. A flavor that will never leave my lips. But it has been long since I tasted her. She is happy?"

"Good. Yes, she is good. She is perfect. But you know I cannot tell you. She would kill me." Even in his fear, Carlisle could feel the joy at the thought of her. Again came Alcibiades' laughter, full and deep. Carlisle was confused: the mother of the Tricksters and the Queen of all Order—how could they share this same man? Alcibiades was lying. Carlisle could not think straight. This could not be true.

"Yes, she would likely kill you. There is nothing better than a dangerous woman. But I did not ask you if she was good or perfect or dangerous. I asked if she was happy. I know she is far from good and very dangerous. Love means I only care that she is happy. You know, I would have traded you—information about Griselda for information about your sister. Hempel is finding ways to be happy. She still wishes for a way to understand how you betrayed your fellow Chosen. But if you will not tell me about my dear lady wife, I fear we must move on."

Carlisle grew quiet. It had been many years since he had been an apprentice to the Raven Sword Master. Many years since he had met his sister in combat under a desert sun and barely left with his life. Alcibiades continued to speak, and as he did, he began to gently tap his spoon against the copper bar, the slow echo like a heartbeat as his words poured out of him. The tap-tap oddly punctuating his every other word.

"The time has come around for my gratitude. First, you came. Thank you for coming. I doubt you will find, in the end, that you would have preferred it, but you have done it. That has turned out very well for me. I was content with one enjoyment tonight. An enjoyment that will now get to change." Alcibiades bowed his head as if to acknowledge the man beside him. Carlisle's eyes narrowed.

"Second, silly boy, you have brought the sword with you. It is a lovely gift I will enjoy giving. A young lady I enjoy the stewardship of shall want it, and her smile yet to be is all because of you." He gave his own smile with a flourish, as if giving a preview, before pointing at his neck and continuing in his jaunty tone.

"And lastly, you see the collar. You removed it. Kay was right, of course. Sweet, beautiful Kay. A girl I dream of seeing again just once in my old man's heart. The collars of Uazit are a source of power. They give unique gifts to all their wearers. Made unique for each Chosen. The jade collar—it was made for me specifically." He pointed inward as he completed the thought and then raised his hands as if to show them dancing around him as he continued. He began to punctuate his every phrase with small, humored laughs as he continued.

"As you may not know, I once lived free across the entire world. I danced from enjoyment to enjoyment. My actions upset Griselda. But Uazit—she did not care. And, well, she liked the violence. But she realized I was a little out of control, even for her, when I got another pregnant. It does not matter who; Griselda and Uazit were the loves of my life. But I lived free. I guess it upset them." He waved his hand before him as if sweeping away his wives' anger from the air. His demeanor turned from conspiratorial to factual, though. He leaned over and looked deep into Carlisle's eyes.

"She had other Chosen before this set, you know? I am sure you heard they all died. They came to stop me from seeing my child be born. But they were silly things, slowing me down. So I put them down. She did not like that. She did not leave me like Griselda did, though. Griselda and her violence, I could appreciate. With time and blood, it may have blown over."

He laughed a rueful laugh. The spoon tapped once on the counter and then spun, slamming into Carlisle's wrist and twisting. Carlisle could hear his companions charge in as he leaned forward in pain. The cracking of the bones in his wrist filled his everything. The world darkened to a pinprick and then refocused. All Carlisle could hear—his perception narrowing again to a pinpoint, narrowing to that spoon as Alcibiades twisted it again and ripped it out of him—was the man's quiet laughter. Carlisle could not help but worry that the man might have severed his hand with a spoon. Blood poured out upon the table, and he felt faint.

"Stupid fucker, I am not a Chosen. The jade collar was

built to chain me and bury me in history. To control my actions

and keep me from ever killing again. Collar me to keep her

Chosen alive and keep me at her bosom. Those children aren't

yours to threaten. Those children are mine." The wild animal

beside Carlisle spun into action. The others in the room first

charged in, then began to scream. All the world except Alcibiades

began to scream. Carlisle danced into motion, but part of him

knew it was too late. That part commanded that he still had to

fight; he still had to try. The other part of him tried to block out

the constant repeating mantra of the man who was killing them

all in a slow and savage tearing away. The single-word mantra of

"mine."

******

Jamie slammed into the ground hard enough to drive her

to her knees. She was kneeling but surveying as Alex had taught

her. Ready to defend herself from whatever came next. She took

a deep breath and looked around at a standard city street

amongst tall, worn-down buildings. The street had seen better

days, and the buildings were more neglected than not. Weeds

grew up out of the cracks in the sidewalk, clawing their way into

the urban jungle. Jamie was not sure what city she had landed in.

She was not even sure where they were in the world. They could not have gone far. The Travel had not seemed to cover a great distance.

The vision had come in her dream. A wild screaming of images and knowings within her brain. Deep, disturbing visions of her master in danger. She could taste the worry and distress through her power, which could only have bled in from Uazit. And then, the strong pull to this location. The feeling had driven her, in a frenzy of obsession, to gather the whole team and tell them to suit up and rush here. If these were the visions that Alex had from Uazit regularly, the visions he used to guide the team, then Alex was a stronger person than Jamie. The pain of the vision had been like a fishhook yanking out her guts, pulling her here. A hook that had dug in and pulled and pulled while a hammering headache of visions flickered through her head.

The flight had been wind-driven, through a starry night. The pull had moved her faster and stronger than she had ever Traveled before. It was Traveling with a wild abandon she could not even have imagined before it had occurred. The flight filled her with energy and joy, but she felt them drain as she landed, and her emotion amped back up into adrenalin-filled need. She felt her collar begin to cycle up power she could use for both defensive and offensive capabilities, even as the ground still shook from her hard landing.

She was feeling the pull to the dive bar that stood before her, even as her knees unbent to stand. She struggled to resist the pull long enough to survey. To assess the landscape as Alex had taught her. To push against the need to act until the entire team could back her up. The cold night air passed through her, and she felt the team slam down behind her. They were a cold, deadly family of raptors coming down on rabbits. Coming down to protect one of their own, to find Alex. The city street shook with their combined landing, and Jamie heard the pavement begin to crack. Jamie shook with the power that surged through her ruby collar as its siblings came into range. She began to shake harder with the need to attack.

Before any of the team could move, the window before them crashed outward. Jamie's collar flashed bright and crimson while the entire world slowed and the body rolled through the air in a sprinkling cloud of glass and blood. The body slowed and stopped as power surged from Jamie, and she reached out to grasp the moment between moments. The body hung there, suspended in the time between seconds, and allowed Jamie to plan her next move. The body was mutilated. It no longer had a gender or a race. It was a mass of meat and bone broken into its parts and held together by sinew. The shock of it broke Jamie's concentration, and the body slammed into the sidewalk with a jarring bang. It began leaking blood while glass rained down upon the street around it like a rain of clinking stars in a storm.

Jamie recovered from the shock and then moved quickly into a defensive stance, stepping toward the body, only to realize it was only part of a body. She was unable to pull her eyes from the sight. What could have done this? This had been done by a monster. Her master was inside with whatever had done this. She began to truly worry. The vision had told them he was here. He needed them. He was in that bar with whatever it was that had done this.

That thought gave her the drive to pull her eyes away from the mass of flesh and step towards the door. She felt her team behind her, moving in unison, in the pattern their master had taught them. In every movement, they honored what he had taught them. They moved as a well-trained hunting pack. One moved with the other as a fluid and dangerous team.

Before they could reach the bar, the door opened and out walked a man, sheathed sword in one hand and jade necklace in the other. He wore a once-blue suit, now covered in blood and gore. He was shining in the darkness. A beacon calling to everything wild in the night to come to him. The man turned his back on the team and closed and locked the door to the bar. He turned back to Jamie with a blood-covered smile.

Even in full battle gear and with the strength of her collar surging through her, Jamie felt a momentary fear in her guts. Her hands and knives involuntarily rose to a defensive position, and the forms her master had taught her bent her body in preparation for attack. Her mind was confused, but her body reacted as it had been trained. Adrenalin surged, and her collar began to pulse in an attempt to begin a build to power it thought she would need to survive what was to happen next.

Her master, Alex, sauntered toward the team, completely ignoring what was left of the body on the street as he walked past it. He peered into Jamie's eyes and smiled a smile she had never seen her master give before. The blood that covered him was like a dark stain, wet and dripping. Part of her felt her gorge rise; another part felt jealous it was not her covered in the gore.

This was her master's true face. She could feel it down in the animal part of her mind. She could feel that this was who he had always hidden behind his mask of many faces. More importantly, she knew she should be running as fast as she could away from him.

"Jamie, what brings you out on a beautiful night like this?" His tone implied a friendly meeting between confidants on a moonlight escapade. Nothing important, not a single undercurrent of electric tension. He could have been a laughing old friend asking about the weather. His tone threw her off. It said safety and calm. Yet everything else about him screamed that he was about to kill everything around him. The small voice at the back of her head screamed that he was about to burn the world. And her collar continued to pulse, continued to build her power to the point that the pain was agonizing—and yet it built. Alex was her guiding light; her team was her family, and he had given her that.

"Master, we felt the call. We came to help."

"Aw, yessss. Uazit felt the collar removed. She would have wanted you here. Wanted you in case things got out of hand." He smiled a rueful smile and looked at his hands and then at the team. Her team, her family. One by one, he made eye contact with each team member. Slowly and methodically, he let his eyes move from one to the other. He seemed to be assessing them. Weighing them. It was like he was seeing each of them for the first time. He looked back at his hands and snapped the jade necklace closed, looked at it and snapped it back open with a gleeful smile. Jamie felt the scary truth that her master was not a good man.

"But more importantly, she would have wanted you to have this." He dropped the cold, dark sword before her and began to walk away, rolling a cigarette. He seemed to have forgotten them and the sword.

Russ whispered, "The Raven Sword."

It was another shock. Jamie looked at the dark sword at her feet. She had to sheath her knives to bend and pick up the sword. She could hear Nettle let out a sharp command to the team, "Defend the blade. Check the bar."

But in the cold night, as blood dripped from doors and windows, they could all hear their master's cold laugh, filled with smoke and humor. He snapped the jade collar around his neck, pulled his cigarette from his mouth and whispered, "There is nothing alive in there to check, my children, my own Chosen. Let us go home. The fight of the goddesses can rest for a night. A chain has been removed from your lives. The lesson how to remove mine has been learned."

Daniel Hansen

RESTLESS CHANGE

"Lift the sword as I taught you." Hempel raised her own sword over her head in a swift, smooth movement. The blade arced over her head in a form she had used a million times. She stood relaxed, yet everything about the stance said she was ready. This was the universal stance of all swordsmen who told those around them, "Come get some." A stance both aggressive and peaceful. She stood silent, like a statue of a master swordswoman. The great Miyamoto Musashi would have been proud to face off against her. She was a picture of serenity and calm.

Nettle moved forward to mimic the stance—a smooth replica. The girl looked neither worried nor defensive, only calm. The two women stood facing each other as mirror images. There was a beauty in what they were. Masters so seldom found each other. They faced off in a small clearing prepared just for this,

their lithe forms comfortable in the bright sun as they stood—
student and teacher. They were untamed panthers facing off in a
calm sea of jungle.

The clearing they were using was surrounded by pine trees
and hills. It was a dip in the landscape, like cupped hands holding
them. Small green bushes pushed up against the wide-open
space, and small swaths of wildflowers crisscrossed it in abstract
bursts of color. A flat, open sea predominated by green, yet
highlighted with dashes of color. Jamie could not name the
flowers, but she had picked several bunches of them and they sat
before her now.

The green and yellow grass and weeds had been mowed
down in a large circle to accommodate the fighters. The circle
was a killing field in the natural landscape. Large flat rocks sat
around the circle at random intervals, for potential spectators.
They sat empty now, taking in the heat of the sun upon their
moss-covered, dark grey surfaces. This was a fighting arena
grown from the natural world and not imposed upon it.

Jamie leaned against a tree at the top of the closest hill,
watching the two women standing in the grass, her picked flowers
a riot of color at her side. The cool breeze blowing through the
trees brought the scent of pine and cut back on the heat of the
day. That breeze screamed that wild days were ahead. She

twined the flowers together, forming little mats of color. They were soft and wild, and Jamie was glad she had started the weaving on a whim.

Joe sat somewhere to her left, enraptured in watching as well. He had a small camera that he used to snap a few photos. He had been using it on and off for a while now and seemed to take great joy in capturing images of everyone. To Jamie, not all scenes seemed worthy of capture. Most were simple representations of life around the estate. He snapped walls and doors at angles that seemed boring and uninteresting. Jamie understood his wish to capture this scene, though. The day was perfect and the women beautiful.

The sun sparkled through both women's dark hair, and the glint of it off the blades conveyed a feeling of power. Two lithe forms facing off in violent confrontation. This was a moment worth capturing. A memory worth savoring for a lifetime. They were so different, these two women. Their dress and mannerisms clashed against each other, the look of reserved tradition facing unfettered modernity. Different, yet mirror images of beauty and violence. Jamie could taste the confrontation brewing upon the grass.

Hempel was dressed in loose slacks and a long-sleeved shirt that swayed gently in the breeze. Its decorative high collar and long cuffs stood out against the homespun wool. Her perfectly shaped short hair curled around her face and tickled her ears. It was a mess of curls, yet every strand looked painstakingly placed. The birthmark along her face and neck seemed to swirl like dark brown henna and highlight the smooth beauty of her caramel-colored skin. She had a classic beauty set against the backdrop of the sun. Her high cheekbones highlighted her eyes and exquisiteness.

Her look was one of tranquility. Nothing mattered but the acceptance of this one moment. There was no tension, just peace. Her body assumed a stance with no effort, and the wind that touched her seemed to dance through her clothing and along her body. The entire effect was one of light and airy calm. The sword she held was a sliver of mirror in her hands. Jamie could see her own reflection in it, even at this distance.

Hempel's feet were bare, and her toes seemed to grip the grass. Barefoot was a state she shared with Nettle. One of the few aspects of her look she shared with the younger woman. In contrast to the reflecting light of Hempel's sword, Nettle held the night sky in her hands. A dark, thin blade of captured smoke made into steel. The glint of the sun off the edge filled the entire surface with cracks and specks of light. She held the Raven Sword.

The sword drew the eye, it was true, but then so did the wielder. Nettle wore a sports bra and tight athletic shorts, both black. She looked ready to enter any modern-day octagon and pummel her opponent. Jamie had looked away when she had first seen Nettle this morning, because the sight had given her an uncomfortable warmth. Nettle's long black hair was loose and wild around her face. It matched the feel of unrestraint that emanated from her frame. Even in her stillness, the energy of her recklessness filled the space around her. Jamie could not help but watch. They looked like two different species of swan floating on a still pond.

The women's sudden movement was a wave crashing against the clearing. Like any sudden flash flood, it came out of nowhere. In a second, the peace of the day was broken by the sharp clash of violence as the swords struck against each other. The swords, like lovers in a primitive dance, jumped first forward then back, striking against each other then circling and starting again. Sparks flew as they struck over and over in a whirlwind of slash and parry. The women were dancers on a stage, whirling through forms and movements, often too fast for Jamie to see. They were a blur of light and dark, leaving tracers as they passed. They circled first left then right. There was no sound from the two women besides the metal-on-metal shriek of the swords clashing. The entire thousand-step movement spun out over moments before the two women separated, each landing feet apart as they stood again in still tranquility.

The warm sun kissed their skin as they stood quietly staring at each other. A moment of serenity before they launched again into combat. Some people create art in this world; some people are art. These two women were art. This moment in the world was art. Two hummingbirds could not have put on a more stunning show. The dance they created was a constant stream of beauty and violence upon the field. They were masters at their craft and weaved together a tapestry more intricate than Jamie could ever hope to match with her wildflowers. It was a dangerous serenity, and Jamie thought it was such a relief after the two weeks since they had returned home with Alex.

Homecoming had been different. Everything had felt different. Alex had disappeared as soon as they had gotten back and had rarely been seen since. The few exceptions were when he was here and there, walking amongst the estate's trees and gardens. And at one point at breakfast, to inform them that Hempel had taken over their training for a time. He also said that she would play a key role in teaching Nettle the uses of the Raven Sword.

All the times Alex was out and about, he never seemed to be hiding from anyone. When he was spotted, he was walking in the open, with no furtive looks or secretive stances. If anything, he seemed to almost bounce as he walked and to take a certain joy in the world around him. He had always seemed to enjoy life, but this joy was new, almost bubbly. Laughter often flowed from him. But something about him was unapproachable. The joys he was experiencing were meant to be private, which was fine, as the team was not ready to smell the flowers with him.

The team was on edge. A feeling of discomfort pervaded the entire estate. They had seen their master in a new light. He was the same Alex—the same intense simplicity they had always known. But now, the monster they had suspected lay within had shown its face, even if only for a second. It had been unnerving. The level of violence he had perpetrated with glee was like nothing any of them had ever seen. It was not that he had killed. They had all killed. It was the fact that the body had looked like it had been torn apart with bare hands. It was the gleeful glint in their master's blood-covered face. Their mild-mannered master was a mask for a creature that was seemingly quite insane.

The team had discussed it at length, going over what they had seen in the short time they had been on the street. The look on his face, the sound of his laughter. The mauled body on the ground and the blood dripping from the windows. It had been a scene from most people's nightmares. It had created a yearning in them, a discomfort they were not sure how to deal with. Jamie kept playing the scene over and over in her head. What had bothered them all the most, without anyone saying it, was the fact that someone had removed his collar. Jamie involuntarily touched her collar at the thought of it. She could not imagine living without it.

They spoke in hushed tones, at once awed and fearful. They seemed unsure whether they should be proud that this was their teacher or afraid of what he might do. Fear was such a new feeling for all of them that they were unsure how to deal with it. Who should they be afraid of, or what? This was a new world. In the end, they needed to readjust their view of their current reality.

It had been María who had finally silenced all debate in an angered response to Joe's worries. "We all knew why we were here. What we are. How many times have each of us killed? He is our master, and he has taught us to move forward in lives that would have ended in pain otherwise. We would have never been accepted outside of here, and he gave us that. He gave us acceptance. Had anyone else ever given any of you real acceptance for what you are before he did? He found us without a way to move forward, and because of him we have moved forward. He taught us. He gave us a home where we could be us.

Where we could be more of what we are. He gave us Uazit, our power. Would we betray him now, for no other reason than that he is more us than we are? And for who—that Carlisle? He killed Hempel's family. He tried to kill us—how many times? He was on the other side. Alex is on ours. Alex is ours."

And so, the weeks had passed and things had reverted slowly to normal. Well, their style of normal. Lessons, sparring, and living-style normal. That normal had led Jamie and Joe to follow Nettle to the outside clearing to watch her spar. Jamie had claimed that she wanted an outside setting to better practice her power. It was true that she preferred to use it outside. There was something pure and comforting about being out from under roofs when she embraced the lightning. But it was no coincidence that her perch atop the hill had the perfect view to watch Nettle's lesson, or that she kept touching her cheek in happy memory. She could lean back with eyes closed and imagine a warm hand in place of her own.

The click of Joe's camera filtered through her thoughts. Jamie looked over at him. He leaned over his laptop, long hair curtained down his face. His camera was sitting next to him, and he reached over a few times, unconsciously touching it. He looked up at her and meekly smiled, then looked back down to start typing again. He was a cute kid, having just recently hit a growth spurt and getting his height. He did not have the shoulders of Russ, but what he lacked in bulk he made up for in wiry athleticism. He had what Jamie had heard referred to as a swimmer's body, which his loose clothing often hid. She threw a handful of wildflowers at him and laughed.

He looked nervous about whatever he was typing, his fingers furiously tapping against the keys. Whatever he had read, he was not happy about. Jamie smiled over at him and then looked back down at the field, where Nettle was on the ground. She lay on her back, looking up. Hempel was on the downward arc of a jump, her sword out, flashing down as if to strike. Nettle flipped up in a move that looked like an undulating snake, snapping to her feet, sword up to catch the descending blade on her own. She shoved both blades up in a sharp snap before driving her foot into Hempel's knee and using the momentum to run up the other woman's body before kicking at her face as she backflipped away. Nettle's kick never connected, but the move successfully separated the combatants and put Nettle back on her feet, with space to move.

Nettle brought her sword up in a back-facing cross-hold across her body as she lowered her stance. Hempel stepped back, raising her own sword and holding it upright in front of her. They circled slowly, testing here and testing there. Hempel spoke loud enough that even Jamie could hear from up on the hill. "Alex brought me here to train you—starting, what?"

"Three years."

"Three years past? You were good even then. But then, you had been alone with him at that point—how long?" Nettle's silence was her reply. "You know you are the last student he ever trained in combat? You were his student until Uazit requested me. I have spent so much time training you, and yet I see who he once was within your movements."

Jamie felt a shock at the conversation. How long had Nettle been alone with Alex? She had never mentioned the tutelage he had given her before the others had come. He had shown her how to fight? Jamie had thought he never showed anyone how to fight. Jamie had always assumed that Nettle had been here with both teachers. But here she discovered that Nettle had spent time with just Alex. Had she known that he was capable of such violence? If not, was she more surprised than the rest? Jamie began to play with the timeline in her head. Assuming she had not lied about when she was picked up, Nettle had basically been raised by Alex.

The sparks below her pulled her from her thoughts as sword struck sword in a fiercely beautiful display of violence. They struck again and again in swift, elegant movements. But they were slowing down, ending the day. Both had cuts and were breathing hard. The sight of them was a warm distraction in Jamie's stomach. The two women bowed to each other and turned off the field.

Jamie clambered up, knocking wildflowers across the grass, and gathered her weavings. Joe put his things into a bag, and they walked down to meet with Nettle. She had the Raven Sword strapped to her back and a towel over her head. She was sitting on one of the large stones, lighting a cigarette. She was vigorously drying her hair of sweat, puffs of smoke dancing from her lips, as the two joined her.

"Wow, Nettle, that was awesome." Joe was a bright star bouncing along in the wake of his hero. Jamie could not argue with his words. It had been awesome. Joe sat next to Nettle, and Jamie stood in the grass.

"Yeah, well, now baby needs a shower." Nettle stretched her arms then smiled up at Jamie. "Too bad I can never reach this one point on my back to get it clean."

Jamie blushed and looked away to the sound Nettle's throaty laughter. Without thinking, she threw the tapestry she'd woven at Nettle in the same playful way she'd thrown the wildflowers at Joe earlier. But rather than ducking a mass of buds raining down, Nettle caught the weaving one-handed and looked at it. She smiled a little smile and jumped up, catching Jamie by the wrists and moving her with a cross-handed throw into the grass of the meadow.

Jamie hit the ground hard. The grass felt brittle as she lay upon it. She turned to see Nettle laughing and bouncing away as she threw her head back and forth like a rock star. Jamie was up and charging after her in a second, but Nettle turned and sauntered away. Joe caught up his face covered with a smile and he sauntered away with Nettle, both mocking Jamie playfully as they went. Jamie caught up with them, and they went from a walk to a race. The race lasted all the way back to the estate before they separated, with promises to join up later.

Jamie wandered the halls for a bit, munching on an orange and thinking. The estate was huge. The out-buildings were greenhouses, storage, workshops, and at least one temple. Large and small meadows intersected with trails and gardens in an encircling maze of trees and nature. The deep river poured past, cutting through the mountains and hills that lay in every direction.

Within the main building of the estate, the entire edifice seemed to have been built at random, with no real rhyme or reason. Hallways and rooms spun off in multiple directions, sometimes with purpose but usually with none. Many rooms were a mix of decorative styles and seemed to have been designed by a madman. The sheer size of it was overwhelming. Jamie could have wandered for years and not seen the entirety of the building, as stairwells twisted down into the earth and up into the sky.

She wondered what it had been like for Nettle to run up and down these halls when it had just been her and Alex. Had she found excitement in the constant exploration, or had she been lonely? Jamie could not help but think of Nettle, about the heat that appeared on her face whenever Nettle spoke. She touched her cheek for one fleeting minute before heading to Nettle's room. She needed to be around her.

Ten minutes of hiking through the hallways later, she sat in Nettle's room. Jamie cleaned Nettle's cuts from the sparring as Nettle pulled smoke into her lungs. Hempel was taking no chances by holding back. Her goal was to ensure that Nettle and the rest were at peak performance, and if that meant a little blood and bruising, then so be it. Nettle did not seem to mind as Jamie gently swiped with cotton balls and disinfectant. It had to sting, but the girl did not seem to even care. Joe was talking about a sword form he had seen Nettle use and was asking about how the style might work against other opponents. The noise was a murmuring in Jamie's ears as she bandaged her friend and looked around the room.

Nettle's room was in no way like Jamie's. There was no set color scheme, as nothing in the room matched. Jamie's monochromatic style was replaced with a riot of colors and disconnected designs. Tables and chairs of different styles and materials were scattered at random throughout the room, and a large brown couch you could sink into was pushed against one wall. There was no bed that Jamie could see, but a long colorful hammock stretched across a back corner, with pillows and blankets spilling out. Ashtrays of all types and styles lay along the floor and tables, empty. How they remained empty with all the smoking Nettle enjoyed was a mystery. The room looked as though a thrift store for pirates had exploded into the space, but something about it was comfortable. For all of Nettle's slinky, over-the-top sex kitten act, the room reminded Jamie more of a deeply eclectic hippie girl. It was as beautiful and as interesting as Nettle was.

There were multiple doors leading off from the room. Many more than the three in Jamie's. She was curious about where they all led and what Nettle hid behind them. But Nettle did not invite her to look around, so she sat on the couch and cleaned the girl's wounds. Joe lay sprawled on a La-Z-Boy-like chair watching the two girls, talking to Nettle, and telling jokes. He turned the camera and began showing Nettle photos of her sparring session on the digital screen. He had captured some amazing shots, and Nettle preened like an eagle seeing a mirror for the first time. She obviously liked to see herself on the screen.

The boy had a good eye, and Jamie was surprised at the quality of the shots. Her own photos looked like blurry imitations of a Claymation world. And she had long ago given up on changing that. It was too bad; she had always dreamed of showing the world her view of it. But it had not been meant to be. She was quietly jealous of Joe's ability and the way Nettle was enraptured by his work. But her jealousy was slight, and she took great pleasure in looking at the images he had captured. She did notice he had a few shots of her weaving the wildflowers. The boy really had a good eye.

Their humor was interrupted, though. A slight beeping hummed beneath their ears. It was the signal for a meeting of the team. As one, they looked toward the door. They moved as a three-person unit, up and around through the door.

They joined the teachers in the dining room. It was brightly lit, and Alex stood at the far end of the room, staring out the window. His back was to the room, and his stance was rigid. Hempel sat at the table, sewing beautiful little decorations onto the high collar of a shirt. After Joe, Jamie and Nettle took seats, María and Russ filtered in after them. The room was hushed and expectant. Alex spoke without turning around. His words echoed off the glass and filled the room with a soft melody.

"There is a Queen we struggle against. It was not Carlisle who oppressed the world. He was merely a symptom. It is She who holds us alien to all that is. She is not our Mother, as dearly as she might desire that title. I close my eyes and dream of her. Dream of it all. She is the hurt that pains us. A memory of things to come. We must be vigilant. We must be strong. There are those who doubt the path I am taking you down. We must be stronger than the doubt that binds us. We must be free. I know this now, in a way you cannot yet grasp. I know we must break the chains that bind us. The Queen and others are wrong. Control is not the way. We must find the places in this world that are free.

"There are areas of this world that are connections to the past. There are truths in the dust of these lands. Wisdom of stone. Whispers of wind. I have built homes in these places and lived upon their sands, surrounded by treasures I collected across the land. The wisdom I left in one such place you must retrieve.

The disc you retrieved is special. One can feel the power if you hold it correctly. It calls out, but we do not know how to answer. I need you to go, my children, go and find a way to answer its call."

ISLANDS OF ILLUMINATION

Jamie touched down near pale blue seas she could see through for miles. The white sand puffed up into the air and cushioned her landing. She could feel the grit of it even through her shoes, and the warm, sun-baked air carried the puffs away in clouds. The bright lights of her team falling to earth lit the sky above her. She reached out and grabbed the moment within the moment. The soft clouds her landing had caused paused in midair like three-dimensional Rorschach tests. She looked up to see her team suspended in the air above her like floating balloons held in place by the string she had seized.

The beach she had landed on was white sand as far as the eye could see along the coast. The ocean was a beautiful blue and green, with gentle waves lapping against the sand. Colorful fish and at least one turtle had paused in this second and effortlessly floated in complete stillness. The waves had stopped just before a crash of white foam on white beach. Above the tideline began lush vegetation and tall beautiful trees. The effect was a green shining in the sun so brightly it almost hurt Jamie's eyes. She had to squint to peer into the depths of that tropical jungle. From her vantage, colorful birds and insects froze in midflight, sparkling decorations sprinkled amongst the trees and palms.

Breathing in, Jamie could taste the delicious flavors of coconut and jasmine. Where their home was all sharp and dangerous, this wilderness was soft and inviting. The estate's trees were thick pines with sharp needles that stabbed into the sky. Their seeds hid away in cones that spiked out. The flowers often had thorns and spines that made them painful to grasp, as if telling the world, "Move it along. Nothing to stop and smell here." As much as she loved her home in Idaho, Jamie knew it for the disagreeable, unstable, and painfully direct—while still mutable—whirlwind of a beast that it was. Here, the land looked soft and calm. The trees gracefully arced into the sky before spreading open long, thick leaves. The palms and ferns along the ground looked inviting enough to lie on. The shockingly bright flowers jumped out and begged to be plucked and smelled. This was a land she could live in—with milk and honey kissing her lips—for years. Jamie wondered, though, was it any less dangerous for all the soft lines and pretty flowers?

Still within the moment within a moment, she could see there was no trail through the jungle. But the mountain range that rose up behind the jungle looked easy enough to reach with a short hike. The range was tall but nothing like back home, so Jamie saw little worry in climbing it if they had to. Most importantly, she had seen nothing of danger around her. No armies of grey-clad villains or their leaders hid behind the rocks and trees of paradise. There were, at this point, only the birds and insects frozen in space.

Jamie dropped the moment and moved quickly up into the tree line. From its edge, the eerie depths looked less inviting than they had from the beach, but still they were soft, still ready. Jamie scanned as far as her eyes and ears could while the whoomph-whoomph of her cohort hitting the sand came from behind her, followed by the crash of waves. The buzz of insects and chirps of birds were broken now by hushed whispers and quiet footsteps as her team took up positions behind her. She turned and looked at Nettle for direction.

The team leader seemed out of place in a jungle, wearing her pristine black uniform. She seemed like she should be a schoolgirl at a school for ninjas rather than in this bright, wild paradise. Of course, it was not like Jamie herself fit, with her thick ruby demon mask and hooded jacket. But then, none of the team would ever likely fit anywhere other than with each other. Look at María in her golden scales. Even with the airy look of it, all that metal had to be heavy and hot, shaped perfectly to her cute young frame. Not to mention that the Stormtrooper and blue Viking looks were not exactly in style. Jamie's contemplation of the team was broken by Nettle's sharp signal to advance through the jungle.

Jamie was the fastest and had the ability to See, so she was the obvious point position. She could also grab moments and assess situations in ways the rest of the team could not. Of course, Nettle had pointed out that it did not hurt that Jamie charged ahead, regardless of orders. Nettle, as leader, followed up behind her, and Joe, with his ability to be invisible, brought up the rearguard. Anyone sneaking up on them would be very surprised when Joe popped into existence and bludgeoned them from behind. The pain of such a bludgeoning was something Jamie did not like to imagine. This left their tanks, María and Russ, to make up the hard-chewy center that could charge forward or back as needed. The differences in how the two attacked gave them a certain diversity of options when they considered how to assault the forces Joe or Jamie were holding in place.

The jungle was thick and hard to press through. On

multiple occasions, Jamie had to slice with her knives just to make a path she could use. She heard the soft swipes of Nettle's sword and the harsh slaps of Russ's ax behind her. The two were so different in sound—the one, a gentle whistling that hummed with deft grace, the other, a percussion of severe slaps like a guttural cry for freedom. Their one commonality was that neither was truly quiet. Jamie wondered how far away the two could be heard as she silently cut through another fern.

The riot of colors and sounds around her started to give Jamie a headache. The musty smell in the air tasted of mold and an old man's bad day. Her thick ruby mask protected her face from the biggest branches, but the open eyes and mouth did little to dissuade insects and dust from choking her and making her eyes water. There was just too much to see, and it hurt her eyes and brain to try. She found herself staring at the ground as she pushed ahead, to cut down on some of the major input she faced. But then, she worried about what she might be missing and again looked up and around. These breaks of ground-staring seemed to help relieve the tension in her head, if not her peace of mind.

By the time they pushed their way out onto the edge of a large pool across from a huge waterfall, Jamie was sweaty and irritable, and knew that she had to look ghastly. The waterfall fell from cliffs whose tops she could not see. She could feel the coldness of the pool and could just imagine how refreshing it would be to strip down and jump in. The scent of the land had changed, and it now smelled less musty and more vibrant. The life here was not waiting for its prey; it was actively stalking it.

Jamie took another cleansing breath and turned to see Nettle and the others breaking through into the wide-open space along the path she had created. She felt a pang of envy as she noticed that both Nettle and María looked fresh and sunny, without a drip of sweat upon their brows. Well, María's veil really covered all that, but Jamie could imagine her lack of sweat. That girl stood like she was enjoying a cool breeze. And with all that damn metal cupping her body, it was just unfair that she could seem refreshed. Jamie threw herself down onto a large square rock near the pool.

It was completely unfair, Jamie thought. Didn't people say "African Hot?" That was a thing. Shouldn't she be better in this heat than the other two? But no, there they were, looking like sweet, fresh slices of lemon pie waiting in the fridge. Damn them, anyway. Jamie remembered hearing her grandpa talk about "Vietnam Hot" and kids at school mention "Mexican Hot." So maybe she wasn't special, and Europeans just thought everywhere not snow-covered was hot. This only gave her mild comfort, until she saw Russ huffing and puffing in his fur vest, with thick sheens of sweat along his bare arms and face, at which point his appearance became a full-blown salve that comforted her. It made Jamie smile, until Joe popped into existence behind Russ, looking even more refreshed than the other two girls.

Joe had a habit of running without his helmet unless he was entering combat, and Jamie wondered if she could do something similar with her mask. She slid it up off her face and let it rest on the top of her head. It held there like it was made to do it. How much of it was design and how much just her desire shaping it through her power she was not sure. The cool air that struck her was an immediate relief, even as she knew they could all see her sweat-bathed features clearly now. Not exactly attractive, but the cool air was worth it.

The hard rock beneath her must have looked comfortable, because the others all found their own, except for Nettle, who stood in the middle of them all. It was a relaxing feeling to sit near the pool. Watch the insects dance along the water. The birds filter through the trees. The squawks and squeaks of life punctuating the steady rumble of the waterfall as it reverberated around them.

Nettle was pacing, but Jamie just enjoyed the moment of rest. She could build a home here and live for a lifetime, just watching it all. It was the perfect place to just enjoy moments, a similar feeling to sitting at her window, staring out at the world.

"Where do we go from here?" Nettle's question was a valid one. Alex had told them almost nothing, and they had very few clues besides the fact that what they sought was "in some caves over around that one place." Alex was a great teacher but maybe not the best at giving directions. They were supposed to be looking for an old building with a map that would help them find the way. But there was no building around. Jamie still had a feeling that they were right where they were supposed to be. The sun beat down, cut by the cool mist from the falling water.

Nettle paced for a good ten minutes before looking accusatorily at her lazy teammates. She stopped then, turning around and around, catching each in her gaze. She stopped and just stared at Jamie, making Jamie nervous, before she ran over and knocked her off her rock.

"Damn it. Get your own, girl," Jamie had tried to say, but the ground reached up and slapped her silent before she finished. She had jumped back up onto her feet before the ground could get comfortable and turned to face Nettle. Nettle was silently digging weeds and vines from around Jamie's rock. Once she had cleared it, she began to laugh.

"This—this is the building." The others looked at her like she was crazy, an assessment that Jamie was ready to agree with until she saw just how smooth a square the rock had been. She got down next to Nettle and could see the outline of shapes carved into the stonework. She looked around at the circle of rocks, the perfect circle of rocks. Then, she started to help Nettle pull up areas of earth to find the flagstones underneath.

It took several hours and pulled them well into noon by the time they had unburied what was left of the stone structure. They were all covered in dirt and grime, and they shared long, lustful looks at the pool. They needed to complete their task before they could think of using the water to cool off. They had uncovered the ruin of a building, bare stubs of columns sticking up where long ago they must have stood tall. The remnants of a roof they carefully laid to one side as the designs carved into the floor started to take shape.

The design was long, flowing lines randomly drawn around the floor, all of which were contained inside an oddly oblong shape that the carver had made no attempt to keep straight. Instead, the outer lines snaked here and there in a large scribble before coming full circle. Inside this oddly shaped container were more lines that covered it in zigzags and shapes. If the design had been on paper instead of stone, Jamie would have dismissed it as one large, random doodle, but someone had painstakingly drawn it onto the floor.

It was Russ who finally figured out that the drawing was a map of the island, and it took the rest an alarming amount of time to see it even once he had pointed it out—the uneven coastline curving around the mountains, surrounded by jungles and hills speckled with waterfalls and pools. The temple itself was represented by a piece of jade inlaid in the stone and darkened with age. They began to look for other areas on the map that might represent the caves they sought.

The green sparkle of jade tinged with red veins finally caught María's eye as they all kneeled upon the design, each brushing away the dirt of years to clear the path. By the look of the map, the spot they sought was near the top of the waterfall. They brushed away a bit more dirt to make sure no other important features of the island were highlighted on the map before they went out to look at the mountainside.

It was not a mountain, so much as a wall of rock that shot up farther than the eye could see from their vantage point at the base. It had looked so small from the beach, yet the water rained down from above in a long steady waterfall. They could make out no stairways carved into the rock or any other method of access other than a straight climb up the face to the left of the falls.

Without another option, they began to climb. Jamie considered, as she hung over a drop that would likely break some bones, why she did not attempt to Travel up the mountain. Alex had said that Travel was the first skill taught, as it could be controlled over short distances. But she was not sure she had the aim or control down yet. So she climbed with the rest of them.

She could feel the heat of the rocks through her gloves and the tightness of most of the handholds. The bugs began to fly around her after she was about forty feet up, as the sweat was really starting to build. She reached out to grab an outcropping of rock, only to have it slip out of the cliff face into her hand, and she hung there one-handed, looking at it. She hefted it as far out as she could so as not to hit the others and then used the hole the rock had pulled from as a handhold.

It took her four hours to reach the mountain top and for once, she was not the first. Joe already lay panting a few feet back as she clambered up and over. She felt a minute's irritation that he did not offer a hand up, but as the others started to come over the edge, Jamie's rubber arms told her why. They all lay there a while, getting their breaths back and relaxing their tired arms and legs. They had a strenuous workout regimen, but nothing had prepared their muscles for this type of exertion.

The view from the top was phenomenal. The fact that the mountain sheared off into the low rolling hills of the jungle all the way to the ocean meant that the view was unobstructed all the way to the horizon. Jamie could almost imagine she saw the curve of the earth out in the water. She shook her head and stepped away from the edge. Too much beauty could hold on like a grasping claw until it hurt you. Jamie needed to ensure that they could make it to the caves. They had already used up a lot of the day, and unless they wanted to practice the camping skills Alex had taught them, they might want to move.

A thin, snaking trail meandered from the cliff face back into the mountain range. After the lush jungle below, the barren rock with short, anorexic bushes was a desert. But the trail was easy and well-cut. It dipped down between rock faces, and soon they were walking under the threat of falling rocks from either sheared side. The rock went from brown-and-grey stone to a deep reddish as they sank deeper and pushed farther. A few veins of white and gold shone along the edges, but they were the only thing to break the monotony of red stone around them. Jamie looked up several times to see the thin, snaking blue of sky that hovered above the deep, narrow ravine they hiked.

Despite the limited color scheme and highly repetitious nature of the formations, Jamie found a quiet beauty in the landscape. The sun struck high up on the cliff face and refracted down around them in a subtle shifting of light and shadow. She was calmed by the hike and almost did not notice when it did a complete U-turn to the left and the blue sky slipped into memory.

The cave they entered was a continuation of the trail, but as it turned back and continued down, Jamie could imagine they were under the earlier parts of the trail. They each used their power to create a space of light around them, though María and Joe, who were the brightest, moved to the front and rear respectfully—which meant that María went to the front and Joe went the rear; respect really never came into it. They continued down, with Jamie between María and Nettle.

The breathing of the two girls echoed around Jamie, as did their footfalls and slight scrapes against the walls. She worried that if there was someone waiting in the depths or following, they would be easy to hear, but there was nothing she could do about it. The stone walls became crystallized in bright spots of color that refracted from María's golden light and seemed to fill the world with color. The trail opened into a large room the size of the hall back home, but instead of polished wood and stone, this room seemed to be carved from jade.

María's golden light revealed tables and chairs and decorative flourishes randomly carved from the floor, walls, and ceiling. The entire thing was one huge piece that must have taken generations of carvers to perfect. Every inch was carved in intricate scrolls and designs that seemed like writings and pictures, but only a few lines came together in Jamie's eye as an actual image. That is, until she heard Nettle gasp and saw that the girl was looking up.

Carved into the ceiling was a massive work of art. Its overarching form was of a man holding a baby. Long, thick lines stood out against the dark background. The man had a look of beatific joy on his face that was a complete image on its own. The infant was laughing, with its arms out as if to grasp the world. The work of art did not end there, though, as the lines of the major work incorporated smaller images. What seemed to be scenes from a childhood danced along the man's shoulder, and teenage years wrapped up the back of his neck. The entire work was carvings within carvings within carvings. It appeared to be the story of the man having and raising a daughter whom he obviously cared for deeply. It was a simple story, yet important enough to someone to have been carved meticulously over what must have been lifetimes. The whole room was a work of art. Jamie felt amazed that they had been able to accomplish something so perfectly, without a single visible flaw. Who would do this, she did not know.

There were hallways, stairwells, alcoves, and rooms leading off this main hall in a haphazard fashion that made little sense to anyone other than to the mad creators. It reminded

Jamie of home. They followed a long hallway of solid jade away from the main hall, in the hopes of finding what they had come for. Once they broke away from the main hall, it became apparent that there were rooms of all sorts of precious gems and metals that called to them from the edges of their jade road. They decided to stick with the trail they were on for a time and see where the jade led them.

It led them, deep and curving, past rooms that pulsed with their own light and rooms that spit darkness out at them. There were rooms of large galleries where the paintings were carved into the walls and statues were one with the pedestals that grew up out of the floors. Until the library, they saw nothing in the entire structure that was not part of the single piece of art that was the structure. The library had beckoned, but the white quartz of the shelves veered away from the jade hallway they had agreed to follow. Still, Jamie made a mental note of its location.

The day was long, but their walk was longer, and Jamie was sure that sunset must be falling outside, even with the long tropical days. Their walkway eventually opened into a large room with a waterfall coming down opposite the entrance and falling into a large pool that took up the center of the room. The jade was carved into jungle trees and ferns with a few birds and animals peeking out. It looked like a green tinted jungle. In fact, it looked like a green model of the jungle they had just left. The level of detail was amazing

Jamie looked around and around and finally walked partway into the pool before she spotted the temple. It was surrounded by hand-carved trees and beauty. With a hoot and a jump, she waved over at it, and the rest of the team soon joined her at its base. The temple was a simple affair, more like an open-air house than a temple. Long, straight columns reached up to a capped roof that hung down over the structure. The inside was comfortable, with a fireplace to one side and odds and ends spread around inside.

The single room of the structure was the first really lived-in room they had found. The chairs seemed to have been comfortable before they had rotted away, and the jade tables and shelves held an assortment of different personal items. A back wall was filled with thin tablets of stone. Jamie walked across to look at them. Alex had said the information would be on tablets just like these.

She stopped in her tracks near the center of the room. The enter team stood frozen. The floor was covered in markings, much like the outdoor temple had been, but this was an intricate recreation of the island in colorful gems and crystals. It sparkled up from the ground in the light of their power. The realism of the depiction was beyond what should have been possible with small, round objects. It was a work of pointillist art that glittered as though it lived. Several areas of the island had man-made structures, and a small village even had little, round people. But the real glory was in the mountains and streams and jungles. Jamie wondered what had happened to those structures, to those people. The island was deserted.

It took a force of effort for Jamie to stop tracing lines with her eyes and get back to the task at hand. She was the first to start pulling stone tablets out and looking through them. They seemed to be an eclectic assortment of knowledge. Alex had said that he had left caches of information in special areas of the world, and this must have been one of the caches he had spoken of. Why the information was on stone and not paper Jamie was unsure, but the thin slabs of rock were carved with minuscule writing and pictures that each told a story or explained some idea or object. Jamie sorted through about thirty of them before finding one with a picture of the disc. It was carved with such skill that it looked like a photo on the page, and the entire tablet was covered in a script too small for Jamie to make out. She could tell it was no language she could read, which meant it was anything but English.

She handed the stone tablet to Nettle, who took one look

and tucked it down the back of her skirt. Jamie continued to sort through the library to make sure they missed nothing. She saw a lot of oddities but nothing more about the disc. After giving up on her search, she wandered the small, lived-in temple, looking at the many odds and ends. An old horn pipe sat next to the fireplace, as though it had been forgotten after a long smoke near the flames. There were plates, pans, pots, and bowls made from a dark black clay that looked well-worn and used. Jamie loved this room, the more she looked at it. It was a simple place to be a simple person.

It was time to go. As they exited the temple, they saw the trail back to the hallway, only now the trail circled back after a few yards and stopped near the pool. There was no doorway to be found. They looked around, but the entire room was surrounded by smooth, carved walls. They checked and double-checked as each of them circled the room and its smooth, flat interior. Joe even did one circuit without removing his hand from the wall, guessing that the doorway was camouflaged in the carved mural of jungle that adorned the walls. This, too, proved fruitless, as the door seemed to just be gone. Nettle stood where they thought the door had been and disappeared into black lightning. She reappeared a few minutes later, claiming that the jade went back at least seven feet, the farthest she had felt safe to go.

They reconvened around the pool, staring dejectedly into its depths. How the hell were they going to get out of there? The door had been there. Obviously, they had gotten in. There had to be a way out. The fall of water cascaded down. On a whim, Jamie decided to determine where the water was falling from. This necessitated a climb up the slick jade wall, using the carvings as foot and handholds. She made it to the top and hung from the ceiling but found only more stone that the water seemed to seep through or build on like condensation, no big hole in the ceiling they could escape from.

She hung there from the ceiling and looked around from this vantage. She climbed hand over hand out from the edge to get a better view of the green world she found herself in. The illusion of jungle was complete from up here. The light from her team was concentrated near the pool's edge, and eerie shadows danced around the walls, the way she imagined they would in a real jungle. The darkness of the room felt more total up here. Down among the group, everyone's light had filled the space and made it feel like a lit room, but up here—up here, she could see the room was much too big for their lights to illuminate.

Jamie's hands and arms grew tired, and she decided it was time to climb back down. Her left hand slipped, and she kicked one leg out, only to realize how silly she must look, hanging over the pool, holding on one-handed, one leg kicking in the air and the other hanging loose. She made a split-second decision and let go. The air around her whistled through her ears and felt like a wind blowing against her. She felt the adrenalin rush she always felt when she fell, and she turned just in time to crash into the water's surface.

The image of throwing a rock into a still pond was classic in the imagery of a single action changing the world—the idea of stillness and stagnation coming to life as gentle ripples spread out from the one action that changed the entire pond. It was an image of peace and harmony in change. Jamie was that rock. She found that her entry into the water was more loud splashes, sputtered water, and a feeling of uncontrolled drowning than it was smooth, gentle ripples. She assumed that everyone had their own perception of the world, and that was fine.

She splashed around in an ungraceful attempt to get her bearings in the water before spotting the pool's edge, now covered in a fine spray and thick puddles. She swam toward the edge, fully feeling the eyes of everyone staring at her. She reached the edge but did not climb out. Instead, she lay there in the water and stared down into the depths, wondering what to do next.

Being trapped in the room was irritating, and the water

weighed heavily upon her clothing. She could see that the pool was carved from the same jade as the rest of the room and seemed to have beautiful fish and water plants carved along the edges. There was even a rise near one side, where what looked like an island might poke out if the water dipped enough. She gave quiet thanks for not having landed there. She looked over at the falls and stopped. The walls under the falls were not all jade. There was a large, roundish area that seemed to be a dark stone instead of jade.

Before she could think about it, Jamie dove back under and swam, this time gracefully, to the falls. She took a breath and dove under again to explore, only to pop up within seconds, screeching for the others. She swam back to shore and waved them over, explaining in a rush that the dark stone was not a stone at all but a tunnel leading away from the room.

They began to talk excitedly about what this could mean or where the tunnel could go. The others began an endless debate about how to proceed. Jamie decided what to do and shared with them the idea that she would go underwater and then communicate what she found. The others had not received her idea warmly, so she ignored the arguments and dove back into the water and through the tunnel, into the dark.

The tunnel was well-carved, just like everything else they

had found, but after a long stretch the jade gave way to rock. The long, smooth walls of a long underground tunnel turned into sharp-edged caves that twisted and turned before opening into a large empty space. The current had pulled her, and Jamie worried about having to swim against it to get back. The water around her was murky, and she kicked this way and that before letting her body go still and float to the top. She was shocked to realize that she did not hit hard rock but open air. She threw herself out of the water in the least stealthy manner possible and began to gulp long draughts of air. She looked up into the bright stars of the sky.

Jamie exited the cool water and pulled herself up, panting, upon the bank. The cold water dripped from her skin and clothing as she caught her bearings. She chirped her coms to let the others know she had made it. She silently gave thanks that Alex had given them this method of communication. Now that she had alerted them they should not be far behind, as the underwater tunnel had been a rather straight, if long, shot at the end. The moon reflected brightly in the pool and illuminated the land around it in a beautiful dreamscape. Jamie could hear low, crawling sounds—the sounds of bodies hiding in the folds and tangles of the jungle around her. She chirped her coms three times, letting the others know she was not alone but also not in a fight.

The land was dark around her, without María and Joe to light it up, but Jamie could tell that it was the same pool and falls near where they had found the outdoor temple. As her eyes continued to adjust to the light, she was shocked to see the blonde woman from the museum sitting in a lotus position at the center of the temple stones. She rested comfortably upon the map. She wore tight jeans and red heels with a long-sleeved, knitted top and vest. She looked like a soccer mom awaiting her children to finish practice. Her heels looked ridiculous to Jamie's eyes, poking up out of the lotus position, but the woman looked serene. How could she come to a fight in a jungle and expect to do well in heels? What was this, a bad B movie?

The blonde woman was the pinnacle of peace and tranquility, sitting there with a quiet look of joy on her face. Jamie had always thought the strange woman pretty, but in this setting, she was gorgeous. The moonlight seemed to sink into her pale skin and gently highlight her hair. She was a goddess there in that clearing, a queen to be worshiped with baskets of berries and jars of wine and honey. The whole moment of entrancement was broken as soon as the woman spoke.

"Do you recall, little girl, the museum? You know I just had to destroy it. I mean, at first I was upset that you had taken my loot. But then, I laughed at the sneaky-sneaky of it all. But it was a place of memories. All those memories being bottled up, held onto, when they needed to be freed upon the world, like little bits of light and laughter to blow away. How sad that memories are allowed to stagnate. Places of memory should be places where you dance, like here. Do you like to dance, little red wagon? I like to dance. Maybe we should dance upon the stones. Is your top here to spin with us?"

"You're a damn loon, lady. You know that? Sitting here in this temple, waiting for us?"

"A temple, you say. Like good little Christians, we stand within our father's home, I suppose." The woman looked at the ground and pursed her lips as if tasting something she was unsure of. "Would they say 'my father's home?'" Again, with the confused look, but it was obvious the question was for herself and not for Jamie. "No, no, maybe right the first time. Those Abraham folk—so hard to quote correctly. Unless you say 'burn-burn-burn.' I guess that always puts on a good show."

The woman's odd rambling was interrupted by the muffled splashing of Jamie's team starting to come up for air. The woman turned to look out over the water as if even in the darkness and shadows she could see the heads break the surface. Jamie knew she had to act.

She struck out at the woman in a standing dive, knives out.

Her knives struck nothing but air as the woman moved without moving and sidestepped the charge. Jamie felt the sharp strike of an open palm against her back, and a second later, she felt the ground as she struck the earth. She shoved up and rolled to the side as the woman's foot struck stone where Jamie's head had been. Jamie flipped up off her back and onto her feet, swiping her left blade out. The woman danced back, barely out of reach, as Jamie stepped in to cut again.

Within seconds of the combat starting, Jamie knew two things. One was that she was ecstatic to have had her blades cut through the woman's vest on one occasion. The blonde had looked shocked and horrified at her outfit's ruination. And two, Jamie had zero chance of beating this woman who was wearing heels and jeans. The blonde moved in a smooth, graceful way that always seemed to take her just beyond Jamie's strikes and just close enough for her to strike back, often in devastatingly painful ways whose ache Jamie could feel. The woman was in almost every way a badass. She almost seemed to be toying with Jamie. At least twice, when Jamie thought she was about to die, the blow struck somewhere else, leaving Jamie to fight on. As the ground struck Jamie again in the face from a specifically sharp throw, she could not help but be thankful that the blonde woman did not ever seem to use weapons.

Jamie rolled to her side in a painful rendition of her roll at the start of the fight. No strike to the ground where she had been ever materialized. She breathed a gentle and sad breath of relief as she realized the blonde had moved on from thrashing her. It was the gentle and sad breath of relief that all broken toys must breathe when the child is tired of banging them against a wall. And Jamie the toy could feel that wall, and she had definitely been banged against it hard and repeatedly.

Jamie slowly pushed herself to her feet in time to see Russ hit a tree in a heavy, boneless crunch and Nettle land hard upon the ground. Neither of them moved quickly after they had been struck. Both were still struggling to rise when Joe slammed into Nettle, knocking her back to the ground in a tangle of limbs and screams. Jamie finally completed her attempt to stand.

The blonde stood facing María. María's mail shone in the moonlight in a dazzling display of glitter. She held out her hand as a surge of lightning struck out, barely missing the blonde, who ducked first to the right then up around flame, hitting the ground under at least three golden missiles before striking María across the stomach. The blonde's fingers cut through the golden scales, leaving four trails of skin showing along María's stomach; they started to well with blood. Lightning struck out from María's clawed grasp, and this time the blonde was too close to dodge it.

Jamie could have jumped with joy as the blonde was launched through the air by the force of the blast.

It appeared that everyone had made the same calculation as Jamie—that the blonde was a BAMF well beyond their current ability. So they ran. The entire team moved as a unit, running from the clearing toward the beach in a mad dash—so fast that none of them saw the blonde land on her feet with a smile. Nor did they see her seat herself again in the center of the stones, staring at the map and tracing it lazily with her finger. What they did eventually see, though, were the grey-clad warriors charging after them, into the jungled night.

None of them stopped or even slowed as they cut through the warriors and felt the sting of cuts and scrapes as knives and branches found them. The run was long, but they had cut the path on their first trip, and something about running with blind abandon through the night sped things up. Jamie hit the beach and ran out upon the water's surface before feeling the weightlessness of Travel take her and whisk her into the sky. She smiled. She had her ass kicked, but they had the tablet. Alex could decipher the use of the disc and answer its call. That was worth her mass of bruises and hurt ego.

LESSONS IN BETRAYAL

Alcibiades was patiently waiting in his favorite chair, looking down at the stone tablet the kids had brought back. He was proud of them and their adventures. They were getting better, and he was impatient to see what they would become. How far they would go. If they would be the warriors to help him burn it all. He set his cigarette on the edge of the ashtray, letting long, gentle lines of smoke curl up from it. The stone tablet was an important step. She would come soon, and he wanted to read what he could before she arrived. It had been lifetimes since he had seen her, so he felt comfortable in his wait, but still he felt a moment's anticipation. He knew she was coming, even if she did not know he knew.

She slipped through the door without a sound. She was as beautiful as ever. He felt a sense of pride, looking her over before she noticed him. She had grown more mature in her look, though age had not touched her. She was attempting a stealthy entrance that, he was happy to see, had lost none of its grace. So many people these days were in a hurry, and she was taking her time. She was a master thief, she really was, and a great source of pride for him. Likely the only source of true love in his life.

Her hair was blonde, cut shoulder-length. Though he knew she regularly changed the style and length, he did like this cut and style on her. His kids called her the Blonde, which he found silly, but he accepted their label, as it was a vital part of who she was. She moved with a jungle cat's grace as she prowled into his room slowly. If he had been any other person in the world, she would have been a ghost, unseen. But he was who he was, so she shone brightly in the night's natural light pouring in from his windows. Again, he felt pride. She was his and always would be. He only wished that he had been able to give her the world. He was disappointed, though, that she had not bothered to reach out and take it—even without him. She was capable; of course she was. He was glad she had come, though he doubted the result would be of benefit to either of them.

"You are still the most beautiful thing in any room, my dear."

She turned with a slow flourish, refusing to show her shock at having missed seeing him when she had entered. She should have known better; he had taught her throughout her formative years. There was little she had as a foundation that he did not know. And even the time spent after being apart would have been a drop in the bucket compared to his long life. But still, he was proud that she covered her surprise so well, never letting it affect her well-trained responses.

"Always with the compliments, huh, Alcibiades? Or is it Alex now? Isn't that what your new kids in the shiny collars call you?" It hurt that she used his name, but he let it go with all the other pains he had ever had in his life. She knew it would hurt; he smiled inside. She moved to sit in the chair he had placed there just for her, across from him. She moved with grace, yet a sense of style so much of the world lacked.

A nice Malbec and two wine glasses sat on a small table between them. Alcibiades poured for them, and stopped himself from filling the silence with the story of the bottle and the grapes. He wanted this silence for a moment. To see her again after so long was a dream come true. She picked up the glass and enjoyed it with a flourish that mimicked his own.

"You have been missed, Kay."

"It was not I who left, Alex."

"You serve the Great Queen now, I hear."

"Should I not serve family?"

His eyes narrowed. "There is no blood there."

"And yet she cares for me like kin, a thing I have not felt in ages. So hard to find family in this world. Though you seem to have formed one in recent years."

"And yet you are not a Champion." It was a statement of fact. It held a hint of his curiosity, but he knew she was not. He also did not wish to follow her particular conversation track.

"I do not wish to be chained. She asked, but I do only the jobs I wish to do. I am not Carlisle to beg or grovel and let her chain me to the cause. I work for the joy of it—and the payment."

"She will chain the world, Kay."

"The only chains I see are the ones your goddess puts around people's necks."

"I received your message. I enjoyed the gift. You enjoy a Kordugum." He reached up and unsnapped the collar from his throat with a low ting that filled the room. He set the jade on the table next to his glass, which he picked up for a drink.

"Can't blame a girl for trying to see her father smile here and there with a gift or two now, can we?" She laughed the same throaty laugh Alcibiades used when he was being sarcastic and truthful all at the same time. He knew his daughter had reason to be upset with him. Uazit had pulled the collar tight well before he had enough time with his daughter. Taken him from her. His daughter had traveled with him for a time. And then with him and Uazit, after Uazit's initial anger had passed and he stood collared. That time had been a blessing and the happiest in his life. Kay had been a blessing.

But then, one day, on the salty banks of some long-forgotten country, Uazit had left them. She moved on, as Tricksters do. Kay and Alcibiades had traveled on, father and daughter, for many years longer. He had taught her greatness. He had shown her the world that would have been theirs to burn if he had been free—until one day, Uazit had pulled the collar tight. The collar that chained and controlled him. He had left his daughter alone in this world. And now, here she sat, being sarcastic and wonderful all at the same time. Her wit was a source of pride to him, and the barbs that stung him just proved her strength.

"Regardless, I owe you for the gift." His words were weighted with meaning beyond their sounds.

"You will let the Queen's people leave with what they have come for?"

"You have come to take the disc, I presume. It is desired

by Your Queen, is it not?"

She raised an eyebrow at his use of "Your Queen" but did not balk. "Can I not come to see my father and his new family? That seems precious enough treasure."

"I will not stop you from leaving. I will not interfere with these people if you remain here with me for a time. A man cannot be blamed for wishing to catch up with his long-lost daughter." He tilted his head as if thinking. "My other children may fight. I would prefer they did not die, Daughter. But when you leave here, our debts are paid. What comes next will be up to them."

A commotion hammered through the building, and Kay took a gentle sip of her wine. "That should be the Queen's people saying hello to your kids with a little surprise visit."

"One cannot be sure how surprised they were. They are well-trained, good kids, and painfully efficient." He made the purse-lipped, squished face of a man rethinking. "When I removed the collar, they would have been alarmed. It might be difficult to retrieve the object you desire." Alcibiades sipped from his glass.

"And yet it is retrieved and leaving with one of the Queen's new Champions. They, too, are well-trained and full of surprises." Her surety filled him with a quiet pride, and part of him hoped she proved as good as she seemed. They sat in companionable silence while the violence continued to erupt outside the door. The wine was good, and the conversation was better.

******

Jamie was awake, lying back on Nettle's couch, the girl's head on her lap as she held up an electronic tablet and read some book. Joe had been kicked back in the lazy chair he preferred in this room, but he had left a few minutes earlier, to retrieve something from his room. Nettle's head was warm and comforting in Jamie's lap. The air was filled with cloying smoke. Jamie could not help but reach down and run her fingers through the other girl's hair. They had sat or lain in just this way a hundred times with nothing but comfort. All five kids had; they were close as a group, and physical contact was often comforting, without stigma or physical attraction attached.

Why this time, Jamie felt the urge for more she did not know, but she did. Maybe it was the feel of silky soft hair, or the woven wildflowers she saw hanging above the hammock. Before thoughts had formed, her fingers were threaded through Nettle's hair, feeling its silky softness slip over her palms. It was a fascinating feeling, and she looked down, just staring at her dark brown fingers entangled in raven-black hair. Her dark skin was beautiful, beautiful as it swirled Nettle's black hair around. It was heaven to feel the tickle of it on the pads of her fingers. And she was lost in the feeling.

"Pull it." Nettle's velvety soft whisper brought Jamie's eyes to her face. Her breath caught for a second at the beauty she saw. The girl's almond-shaped black eyes stared up out of her perfectly shaped face. Jamie realized that there was so much about this girl she did not know—that she should know. She had never asked her even jokingly what part of Asia her family had come from. She had not asked her what it was like to live in Honolulu or how to steal a car. What it was like to be alone for years with Alex, practically raised by him. What her family was like, what surfing was like. All this time and she did not even know the basics. She opened her mouth to ask, and Nettle leaned up and kissed her.

There was no soft, gentle caress of lips, no tentative moment of buildup. This was not young love in a tender story of romance. It was an animalistic frenzy from the moment Nettle's tongue slipped into Jamie's mouth. Jamie's fingers gripped Nettle's hair and held her head aloft. Nettle's own hands reached up and pulled Jamie's face hard against her lips. It was a moment of passion that Jamie would forever taste.

Jamie moved without thought or planning, as neither were possible during this kiss. Nettle pivoted her body and grabbed Jamie's shirt, twisting it in her hand to pull herself around and climb up so she was straddling Jamie's sitting form while deepening the kiss. Jamie kept one hand in the other girl's hair and moved her other down to put pressure on the small of Nettle's back to pull her even closer. She felt Nettle try to pull up on her shirt, but they were pressed much too close for that. The girl tasted of coffee and tobacco. Jamie wanted to drink her down in a puff of smoke.

Nettle leaned back with a sigh and pushed her face down into Jamie's neck. Nuzzling against the soft skin of her neck, Nettle nibbled at Jamie as her hand came up and slid along Jamie's earlobe. Nettle's hot breath danced against her skin, and her long hair tickled Jamie's face. Jamie's stomach tightened as her body reacted. Jamie used one arm to squeeze Nettle against her, and the other hand lifted Nettle's face to start the kiss again. Jamie moaned as Nettle ground her body against Jamie, and she let the other girl devour her with the kiss. There was a driving need for more.

Jamie felt the power building within her and a matching power build in Nettle. Their necklaces pulsed in unison, drawing power from the world and from each other. Jamie slid her hand up the back of Nettle's shirt. She could feel the muscles under her smooth skin, and the joy of that feeling made her kiss Nettle all the harder. Jamie's power danced along her hand and spread against Nettle's skin, creating a burning pleasure that connected them. Jamie could feel Nettle's power light up at the base of her neck through Nettle's hands. Nerve endings fired with raw power and electrified them both as the lightning of their powers began to intertwine in an agony of desire. Their entire bodies became conduits of power and pleasure. The need of it built as they kissed and Jamie yearned for more. It was hunger within her, an immediate addiction.

Nettle pulled back suddenly and left Jamie cold. Nettle looked around as if exploring the room. There was something calling to her, something she had missed. As quickly as possible, Nettle was up and looking at the closed door with her head cocked. She was tense in a different way, and Jamie could not help but appreciate the tight spring of her body as she stood there. Her stance and tension worked to show off every part Jamie wanted to see tense.

"Did you hear that?" Without waiting for an answer, Nettle ripped open her door and charged out into the hallway. Jamie was up and after her, wondering what the other girl had heard. Nettle was halfway down the hallway at a full sprint, before Jamie was even partially across the room.

As Jamie reached the hallway, a shocking vision struck her. Her mind screamed out in images and information. It pulsed and prodded at her like a fiery whip striking her body. The world blackened, and her vision wavered. Alex was again without his collar. Her master was unprotected. What would happen to him without the power they all needed? She veered from running behind Nettle to running toward Alex's room. She yelled out for Nettle but got no answer. Jamie made a quick decision to both save her master and trust Nettle's ability. As she ran, she clicked her throat to talk to the entire team over their personal intercom.

"Alex's collar was removed. Nettle is going after a disturbance near the entrance."

Joe's response was quick. "I will join you in helping Alex. Russ. María. Can you assist Nettle?" The note of command was alien to the boy, but Jamie was glad to hear him finally taking charge.

She turned the next corner at a sprint. As the power filled her, she let it burn away the clothing she had on and create her uniform in its place. The ability to burn away her clothing was a trick she might want to remember for later. She left the knives for last and let these new extensions of herself be created with a perfection few real knives could have ever competed with. She felt like death incarnate. She felt powerful and god-like. She was the demon of her mask.

She turned a last corner at a full sprint—and into a throng of warriors. She dropped to her knees, leaned back, and slid along the smooth hardwood floors between and past the first two warriors. As her momentum started to slow, she popped back up and leaned forward, driving her left blade into the gut of the man before her. Gunfire rattled around her. Her right hand spun out and around, cutting through flesh Jamie did not even see before she charged forward into the void between her two knives. She hit the wall running, slicing through a woman with a gun, and her path curved up the wall about halfway. Then, she ran along it about ten feet before tackling another combatant.

The air smelled acidic from gun smoke as Jamie tackled a man, driving both knives into his chest and letting him fall backwards as she fell with him. As they hit the ground, she let the force of their fall flip her head over heels so she landed on her feet, arms out and feet moving towards a t-intersection. As she cleared it, there were more warriors to the left and Joe running up from the right. Jamie turned to the left and dove in. Her world became a whisper of movement and cutting as she danced amongst the enemy, slicing through them like skis through snow.

Gunfire caused her to lean left and a swinging sword caused her to step back. As she did, the world exploded at the base of her skull. She was driven off her feet and onto her knees under the crushing blow. Stars burst behind her eyes and clustered in her brain. The pain was momentary, yet it devoured her thoughts in an instantaneous singularity. Her hand instinctually pulled back her hood and went to the back of her head. It came away wet with blood and searing pain. Her body wanted to black out, but her mind wanted to survive.

Jamie rolled to the side and spun as she came to her feet to see her attacker. Joe stood there, a glass-like spiked club in his hand. Jamie shook her head to clear the darkness that was trying to take her, but the shaking only caused the pain to reignite. She had a moment to give thanks for her hood and how much worse the blow could have been. She could feel the blood still dripping down her hair. She knew then that the damage done was likely worse than she could fight through. She gave another moment of thanks that Joe was there to back her up with this head wound. She looked over at him.

Blood marred the clear surface of Joe's weapon. He stood like an avenging angel in his white armor. Tonight, he had chosen no helmet, and his long hair hung down loose to his shoulders. No blood marred his ivory; there was only bright red blood along his club. Joe stood there looking at Jamie, flipping a large gold coin in one hand. Jamie realized that the warriors she had been fighting were standing quietly around them, all of them staring at Joe. And it was not so much a large coin he tossed, as a small disc.

Joe laughed out loud and swung his club at Jamie. She reached up to block it, taking the blow on her right forearm. It exploded in pain as the bones crunched and the club stopped. As the club swung back up, it changed into a long sword of glass. Jamie dove to the left and rolled through her landing before a short turn brought her to her feet, facing Joe. "What the fuck are you doing, Joe?" Jamie could hear the incredulity in her own voice. She was confused. Shocked. What was going on here?

"I see you all. Do you know that?" Joe smiled with quietude, yet spoke with accusation. "I see you. You are the monsters here." There was no emotion or feeling behind his words. A truth stated, nothing more. But his voice rose to a near shriek as he added, "I will no longer be a monster." His words became thoughtful and caring. He wanted Jamie to feel the sorrow he was feeling. "I see you—you and Nettle, with your stares at each other. I see you, Russ and María, with Russ sneaking out of her room at all hours. I see how María looks at you. How long before it is the four of you sneaking out of the same room?" He shook his head in sadness. "I see you. I see the way you and María exalt the killing you do." He looked at Jamie with pleading eyes, as if begging her to tell him he was wrong. "I saw you when you struggled with what you were. What we are. I wanted you to see me. But you do not struggle any longer. I see you practicing your power. I see you training. I see you. I see all of you." His voice had risen in accusation and pain as he pointed his sword at Jamie. "I see it all, and every night, I type it up and send it to Her. She sees me. She sees me."

Joe charged at Jamie, his sword raised. Jamie parried his blow with the knife in her left hand. She was starting to worry about how badly her right arm was broken, as she was unable to bring it into play. If she was going to survive this, she would need both of her knives. The pressure of Joe's sword pushed down against her knife, but she held the knife steady.

She looked deep into Joe's eyes and saw crazy looking back at her. During sparring sessions, Joe had never been a match for Jamie, but the kid was quick in short spurts. With Jamie's broken arm and whatever damage that had been done to the back of her head, she was not sure if she could take him. But she was damned if she was going to die by him.

She kicked out at Joe, forcing him backward, and dodged away, slamming into one of the other warriors. She drove her knife into the warrior's stomach—a killing blow, but the man would not die quickly. Jamie used the force of hitting him to spin them both around, like two teens slow-dancing, before jumping up and kicking him as hard as she could in the chest, driving the dying man back into Joe's path. She turned and ran, slashing at anyone that got too close.

The two men stumbled into each other before Joe threw the man aside and ran after Jamie. She could hear his slamming feet hitting the ground behind her. But she had always been the fastest on the team. There were too many warriors between her and Alex's room, so she made a split-second decision that Alex could handle himself but she needed help. She swerved at the last minute, diving through a window and crashing through decorative trees and shrubbery and landing roughly on the ground below.

Jamie was up and running in seconds, holding her arm against her chest. She ran like her body was an arrow her mind had aimed and fired. As she reached a series of out-buildings, she chose turn after turn at random, hoping to throw off anyone chasing her. She never bothered to look back and looked only at random points ahead. But always, always the same point was her end goal. The night had swallowed her pursuers, if she still had any. The light from the front doors shone bright, and she ran towards them.

The doors had been shattered inward in a spray of wood and splinters. Dead bodies littered the area just inside the entranceway. And Jamie could hear commotion inside. She moved up to the door frame and slipped up against it. She peered in at the large main hall of her home and found smeared blood and desolation. Russ' ax was buried into the stone near the door. It stood out like a great blue moon shining with an inner light.

María stood like a queen in her gold-scale armor more than halfway into the room. Her eyes burned through her golden veil. She was magnificent, a dark brown queen wrapped in gold and glowing so bright it hurt to look straight at her. She held pure golden lightning in one hand and yellow flame in the other.

She was fierce and angry, and Jamie could see why. Russ lay at her feet, a pile of blue cloth and painted flesh draped upon the floor like some fainted damsel. Warriors in grey lay spread across the floor. As Jamie watched, María raised her hand, and lightning jumped out, striking into those still standing. When the lightning hit them, an explosion of light ripped from the warriors and filled the air with a mist of power. The bodies struck the ground seconds later.

Jamie lifted her mask as she ran up to María and caught her with her uninjured arm before she could fall. The girl was breathing hard, but not yet ready to collapse. Even still, she leaned on Jamie, catching her breath. The smaller girl was like a skeleton in Jamie's arms, frail and shaking.

They stood there holding each other for several minutes before María leaned in and licked Jamie's cheek right where blood had splattered and bent to check on Russ. He was breathing, and she looked happy with what she found. María knelt over him and dipped her head down and licked blood off his face. It was a moment of intimacy that Jamie wished she could kneel and share. Before she could, María then slapped him across the face. He began to cough, turned to his side and coughed again. María held his head and pulled it into her lap.

"Nettle—she was to meet you here."

"We were outside when we heard the door, heard your call. We came. I did not see Nettle. There were many... The girl in green—she was a hurricane. She hurt Russ."

Jamie tapped her neck and pictured Nettle's face. "Nettle, where are you?"

"I am with Hempel. We are almost to the main hall."

"I am here with Russ and María. Russ is down but alive. Hurry. We are hurt. I do not know how well we can hold off anymore." Jamie looked around the room. The battle Russ and

María had fought was massive. A girl in bright green lay dead, ten feet away, and over a dozen wearing the standard grey of the Order's army lay here and there. Jamie could feel her arm becoming a dull ache as she tried to get herself into a defensive position. Which reminded her... "Nettle."

"Almost there, Jamie."

"Joe. Joe is with them. He is one of them." Jamie made eye contact with María, who looked up at the news. There was silence in the air.

Nettle and Hempel came into the hall in a cautiously practiced way. They took in the sight quickly, if grimly, before approaching the trio near the center of the room. Hempel dropped to Russ and began checking him. He groaned as her hands explored his many lacerations. Nettle and María surrounded Jamie as they all began to talk and Jamie told the tale of Joe attacking her and his theft of the golden disc from the museum fight. She was ashamed but told them about throwing herself from the window then running clear around the estate to reach the front door.

María told them that she and Russ had come straight here from outside when they heard the call. They had unthinkingly dived into a small group of grey-clad warriors before being surrounded by more. The girl in green had appeared from nowhere and struck at Russ. The two had fought amid the rest of the battle until she finally struck him a solid blow along the face, followed by what appeared to be a severe strike to the abdomen, and he had gone down like a sack of rocks. María had saved him from the girl's killing blow with a gold bolt before grabbing the woman by the face and frying her insides with lightning and fire. The rest had been mop-up, which Jamie had walked in on.

Nettle had run into a force led by a giant of a man and had fought for several minutes before Hempel had charged in from the other side, trapping the group between them and cutting them down. They had moved slowly and sneakily after that, in short bursts of speed, peering around doors and corners before attacking or moving on. Their regimented advance made Jamie blush as she recalled flying with wild abandon around corners and through at least one window.

Jamie showed them her arm, and María carefully checked the back of her head as Nettle stared woefully into her eyes and explored the break. The feel of fingers in her hair caused her to clench in pain as María sucked in a worried breath. After the inspection, Jamie had to sit while the team began to regroup and decide how they recovered from the devastating physical and emotional blows they had received.

Getting to Alex was the first step. Russ was sitting up but

not on his feet, so both he and Jamie would be liabilities at this point. Leaving them behind in the hall seemed like the more dangerous of the possible plans; nobody was sure how many enemies were still out there. If they both could walk, they would move with the rest. Jamie got to her feet and held out her broken arm. Nettle held it straight while María made sure the bones were set with excruciating precision. Jamie wrapped her power around and around her forearm until it was encased in a hard red shell that held it and her hand in place. She should have thought of it earlier and saved herself the disuse of her arm. The hard red shell would work as a cast. She then felt her power fix and thicken her hood before she pulled it up over her head and pulled the thick mask over her face.

After the impromptu operation to patch up Jamie, Hempel lifted Russ easily to his feet, and Jamie put the strong boy's arm across her shoulders and allowed him to lean heavily on her. They then began the long trek to Alex's room, through bloodied hallways and bodies. Hempel led the way with the half-moon blades she called ulus out and ready to cut. Jamie and Russ hobbled along together. María walked slightly in front of them with golden spheres in her hands. Nettle brought up the rear with the Raven Sword.

The hallways and rooms they passed were scenes from a

nightmare. Nettle and Hempel had not had an idle walk back. Their home looked like the aftermath of the world's roughest kegger. Bodies, cut and bleeding, leaned drunkenly against walls or over furniture. Several times, Jamie had to steer Russ around a sprawled-out form on the floor. She could not remember which sections of the hallways were hers until they came to the broken window she had crashed through. Bodies upon bodies framed the walkway, laid out like an honor guard. More were piled in haphazard fashion along the floor, in a trail of devastation that led out and through the window.

María whistled from beside her in an appreciative fashion. "You go, girl. Holy shit. You cleared these hallways alone in, what, a few minutes?"

Jamie could not help but feel a surge of pride as María looked at her appreciatively. She smiled, and then grimly pointed out a cleared section with her lips. "There. Joe hit me there. And then we fought, and he chased me through this group here, and here I jumped out the window."

Jamie replayed the scene in her mind. The young man she had come to consider a younger brother laughing his maniacal laugh as he swung his massive weapon at her. The pain of breaking both bones and loyalties ached inside her.

They plowed on, only to find that the rooms and hallways

were now clear. No bodies, no signs of struggle, not even a vase out of place. The entire area was pristine up to Alex's closed door. They knocked, and without waiting for an answer, Hempel pushed the heavy wooden door open.

Jamie had never been in Alex's room. The entranceway was huge. Two fireplaces burned along opposite walls, and the rest of the perimeter was lined with shelves. Books and oddities filled each shelf. More oddities were laid out on small decorative tables. The room reminded Jamie of the museum they had hit. Everything seemed old and seemed strategically placed to be seen. Only a few chairs sat out by the fires. What the chairs lacked in quantity they made up for in size, each one a massive affair of leather and cushioning.

As the main door closed behind them, Jamie realized that the door was also lined with shelves, causing it to disappear into the design of the room. She looked around, realizing that now that the door was closed and hidden, she could spot no doors leading from the room. The one thing she could spot, though, was her master seated before the fire. A small table sat between him and another chair. Several empty bottles of wine and two glasses were set out. Alex smiled as he looked up at them and sipped from a glass. At his throat, his jade collar sparkled in the firelight. "Oh, my. You all look very disheveled. An exciting night,

I take it?"

There was momentary confusion at his words and smile. He must have heard the assault, not to mention the fact that his collar had been removed. But here it was, back on his neck. What had happened here, and how did he seem unaware of it? Hempel reported the attack and aftermath as Jamie just stood there, holding up Russ and staring at the scene. Two glasses. Alex looked contemplative as Hempel, and then Nettle, recited all the facts of the day. Alex never looked surprised, even when they recounted Joe's betrayal. Sad, yes; surprised, no.

"He has made Carlisle's choice, my dear. I fear She is a crafty temptress. I had hoped, in my egotism, that my children would be immune from the Queen's temptations. It hurts to be mistaken." He was looking at Hempel as he said it, but then his eyes roved over the entire team, taking in each person with a practiced, if lazy, eye. He seemed unconcerned yet saddened by what he saw. Another sip of his wine as they all stood around him in silence.

"She is evil," Hempel whispered with vehemence.

"Now, dear, it was a wise man who once said that the truth about evil humans refuse to face is that it sleeps in our beds, eats our food, drinks our wine, and stares out from our mirrors." Alex stood as he spoke and walked to Nettle. He smiled at her as a father would smile at his beloved daughter. He finished his spiel and quieted.

"It cannot be a coincidence that after we get the stone tablet, they come here to take the disc from us." Nettle seemed thoughtful, yet angry.

"My dearest girl, coincidence is the greatest source of human irrationality because of all the minds trying to find causality."

Reaching up, Alex tapped Nettle's forehead. She cried out and stepped back. He then moved to Jamie and tapped her as well. It was a dive into a frozen pond, and she heard her breath hitch and her body tighten. The cold deepened and burned as its suddenness shocked her mind. Her head screamed in pain, and her arm began to throb. She could feel her body unknitting in a painful fashion before reweaving in excruciating ways. The feeling lasted for seconds; it lasted for years. Her body ached by the end of it. Her body was healed when it was over. She looked around, and the entire team was bright-eyed and standing tall. Jamie's arm felt strong, and she could flex her fist. Her master looked at her with the monster's smile. "Now, my children, it is time you remove a few players from the field and kill some bitches."

PAINFUL LESSONS

Jamie landed with a hard crunch upon a flagstone courtyard. The buildings around her were large, square structures laid out in a well-ordered design. Each building was the same size and shape as the others and the same distance from the others. This was a compound built to a plan—a rigid, structured plan that made the whole thing feel industrial. Jamie could hear the calls of alarm, and she immediately sprang into action, diving at a grey-clad woman, knives out and cutting. As she passed the woman, she reached out and grabbed the moment between moments.

The world slowed to a stop, and the blood from the woman's neck froze in mid-spray as the woman herself stopped mid-fall, a look of fear upon her face. Jamie could see the blood on her blades and a single droplet formed and fell. It was the same dark, rich red of Jamie's mask. The drop stopped in midair a foot from the blade as it left the still-turning time around Jamie.

It was the first time she noticed that time kept moving close to her. She counted warriors in the courtyard around her and the ones on the walls above. There were many, but she traced her potential path through to enter the building closest to her left. That was the building she needed to get into to find the disc, to find Joe. The other team members were frozen lights filling the courtyard with illumination as they plummeted to the ground.

Jamie released the moment and charged ahead. The warrior's body slumped to the ground. As Jamie charged ahead, she could hear the team begin to slam into the ground behind her. Falling stars striking rock, the sound of cracking stone filled the air. She kicked a man's leg and used the momentum to run up his body. Hooking one leg around his head, she spun, dragging him off balance before flipping off with a quick snap of his neck. Spinning, body flat, leg out, her foot struck another warrior in the face. She curled her body in over the head of the falling form and then leapt up and off, driving the body into the ground. She came down amongst a gaggle of fighters. She felt a blade bite her skin as it cut through her jacket, and she spun, driving her knife into the body of the offender. She could feel her own blood swell through the wound and cool the sting of the cut.

Amidst the masses, Jamie had to jump and dive in acrobatic twists to avoid blades and make slashes into flesh. Her body contorted around sharp edges as her feet connected to crunching bone. She landed and twisted back before snapping up and driving her blades into flesh. Her backswing brought the knives out and wide in a large circle around her body, filling the air with blood and screams. The more she cut, the more hands and weapons reached for her. She wove her body through the pack like a needle darning a sock. She felt the cuts of those who connected with her, but none of them were killing blows, not like hers. The noise of battle surrounded her as her teammates danced the same dance she did.

Nettle was a blur of darkness with the Raven Sword. She was a flash of night that cut through the world like a streak of black marring a painting. María threw bolts of light that flared and burned through the night air, her outstretched hand throwing golden lightning that burned flesh and struck down bodies. Russ, though, was the bright, shining star in the night. His massive size and swinging ax filled the courtyard with his presence. The bright blue shine of his power was magnified by the swirls of face and body paint that were covered in blood. They each danced alone, and yet they were a team. Jamie took only a moment to look at them before reentering the fray.

She was not sure how many grey-clad bodies hit the ground before the shots were fired. She heard the five sharp claps, and she reached out and grabbed the moment. The scene stopped. She could see the shooters along the wall and other warriors still in the courtyard. Her teammates were islands of beauty, crushing resistance in their own small spheres of paradise. Bodies froze mid-roll along the ground, and at least one had halted as it flew through the air, struck by Russ' ax. The man's head was back, his body bent backwards, legs askew and arms out. Blood and spit froze in the air over him like a red-and-white mohawk. Nettle was frozen mid-sprint as she ran toward the wall. She was lithe and beautiful, in her short skirt and obsidian tights. The tied remnants of the scarf she used to cover her face billowed out behind her, frozen like two waving arms. Despite having downed several opponents, not a single drop of blood marred her obsidian perfection.

Jamie counted the bullets in the air. Three had halted only feet from her. They were bits of lead hovering gently before her. The other two flew toward María to her left. María sparkled in the night, with her gold-covered form splashed in blood, like a dangerous viper that had polished its scales. Each link of mail glowed with light reflected from the lightning striking out of her open palm and into a crowd of warriors. The world around her was filled with a light smoke, acidic to the taste. She was a blood-covered queen, laughing through the veil as she struck out at those who opposed her.

Jamie was moving before time began, and the sound of a body hitting a wall filled the air as she tackled María to get her away from the bullets. The two girls hit the ground in a tangle of flesh and limbs. They rolled together along the ground as the bullets struck stone instead of flesh. Jamie felt the sharp edges of golden chainmail dig into her as the weight of the smaller woman settled into her arms. There was a sharp flash of heat as they came to a stop. Jamie stared down into María's face and saw a deep flush spread under the veil. Bright red lips pursed. She realized that their uniforms did little to interfere with the feeling of flesh pressed to flesh. Jamie wished it was anywhere else and any other time. But violence called all around her, and violence was a beautiful thing.

As she still straddled María, Jamie looked up and saw Nettle complete her run to the wall, sword out. Jamie lifted her mask, in awe of the sight before her. With a sharp leap, Nettle struck the wall and began to run straight up it, sword dragging behind. As her feet hit the top edge of the wall, Nettle kicked up, letting her momentum carry her into a backflip high above the wall, arms out. It was a free-flowing moment of light and violence. She was a floating angel hanging gently upside-down. She completed the flip and her feet reached the top of the wall with a graceful landing that bowed her body to the ground, her arms spread wide like a swan bowing to its mate. She was a ballerina upon the parapet.

Nettle was moving before Jamie could truly take in the full beauty of the moment. María relaxed beneath her, and Jamie looked down to see María staring up, watching Nettle open-mouthed. The heat of their stacked bodies became too much. Jamie climbed up, missing the warmth against her as soon as she moved. The night felt cold around her. Russ was against a far wall, cutting through a tall man as Jamie helped María to her feet. The two watched Nettle run along the wall, dodging bullets and cutting through flesh as she cleared the wall top of gunmen before jumping to the ground. María leaned in with a soft kiss to Jamie's lips through her veil before running towards the few warriors remaining. Jamie dropped her mask into place and chased after her. As a unit, the team ran into the building, ready for war. The taste of gentle blood and violent metal filled Jamie's mouth with joy.

******

Joe flipped the disc in his hand, feeling its power fill him. The blessing of Order filled him. He did not care what Kay said; this power was a freedom, not a chain. He loved it; he drank it in like a long draught of water. This was what he had been missing. Who needed a team when he had this power within him? His white uniform clung to his frame, and he loved the feel of it. It protected him and exalted him above the normal weak soldiers in grey. He walked first one way and then the other, pacing back and then forth around the room. He felt restless suddenly, for some reason.

The room he was in was a perfect square. Decorations hung in long, methodical rows around the room, a mix of carvings and black-and-white photos all perfectly and uniformly laid out. The furniture supplied was placed in well-spaced sections that kept the center of the room empty, which was good, because Joe had an itch that his pacing was not able to scratch.

It was on the eleventh lap that the door opened and Alex walked in. He walked like any other friend strolling along a hallway. The same stroll he had used walking into Joe's room at the compound. A long glass blade was in Joe's hand before the door had silently closed. He charged at his old master, but his sword only struck stone. Joe turned with a flourish, striking out, and Alex stepped back with a small smile. Joe struck again and again, but each strike found only air. Joe was a hurricane of blows and strikes, but not a single cut hit the target.

"You have gotten better, my child." Again, the sword bit into the air as Alex stepped away.

"I am not yours or a child any longer." This time, Joe's

sword hit flesh as Alex caught the blade bare-handed and pirouetted around the boy in a graceful flourish. The blade was neatly plucked from Joe's grasp, his hands suddenly empty. Alex sat himself upon a chair and motioned with the sword to the chair beside him. "You will all always be my children."

"I serve the Queen now. She sees me, unlike you people."

"My child, I found you. I saw you. I see you."

"The Queen will fix the world. I will help fix the world." Joe's voice rose in octave and righteousness. The alarm began to sing outside, and Joe jumped toward the door.

Alex moved without moving. He slipped up and around until he held Joe by the throat, and he threw him against the wall. "There are a few other children of mine. I have sent them on a mission to clear this compound and get me back what I want. But their attack works to distract your guards and army so that we may speak."

Joe was up, a sword forming in his hand. He struck. An attack with all his might, and Alex easily moved past it. Joe swung again, and Alex moved under the blade to tap him on the arm. The fighters moved from left to right. One of them fought hard, with all his might, and the other barely began to breathe hard. Each swing was followed by a light tap. Frustration grew.

As they fought, the older man spoke. "Have you heard of the man Camus? Camus lived in France during the Nazi occupation. He was not what you would call a supporter of the Vichy. He was a young man. Still able to feel a young man's hate. One night, he was picked up by a group of soldiers, who put him in the back of a truck, so they could haul him away to a concentration camp. This was a random choice of prisoner, on the part of the soldiers. They were told to get X amount of people. Camus was on the wrong street, on the wrong night, looking wrong." Each word Alex said was punctuated with sword strikes and Joe's grunts as the sparring continued. Even as Alex dodged and struck, he spoke in a cool, calm voice. Unhurried.

"In the back of the truck, there were twelve other prisoners and a Catholic priest. The priest was there to 'watch over' the prisoners, in the interest of legitimizing the Nazis pulling them from their beds at night. Basically, he had been pulled from his church at gunpoint. He sat in the truck all night, and then got to go home in the morning still alive if he behaved." Alex caught Joe's sword arm and threw him up and through a table with a crash. It was only the second violent response from Alex since he had entered the room.

"On this night, in this truck, these soldiers had argued. They had a quota. They had not yet filled that quota. They took it upon themselves to grab two more people. One was a boy around the age of twelve. The boy sat at the back of the truck, near the gate. Across from him sat Camus, who was the other lucky winner of the Great Nazi Truck Ride. Beside the boy was the priest. Across from the priest was Camus." Joe flipped back onto his feet. The pieces of table and furniture went flying. Alex caught him by the throat and hammered him into the wall. Decorations and wall hangings crashed to the floor. Their faces were inches apart as Alex hissed. "Can you imagine that night? That truck. The fear that permeated all those men. Can you smell it—that fear? Can you see the dirty, unwashed bodies huddling together? Hear their silent whimpers? Taste it, that cloying, clawing fear in the air? Imagine it." The scene was punctuated by Joe crashing into a chair as Alex threw him again.

"That truck hit a bump. Nobody aimed for a bump, but it was hit, nonetheless. The boy fell out and lay in the road. Three people noticed: the man beside Camus, Camus, and the priest. The boy had not attempted to escape; he had merely fallen out. All they had to do was keep quiet, and the boy would avoid the camps. He would live. The soldiers had not bothered to get his name. They would never bother looking for one child. It was dead quiet in that truck, until the priest yelled for the soldiers to stop and go get the boy." Alex landed upon Joe's downed body and shoved him into the floor.

"That priest had a duty. He worked for the Germans, but he had a duty to that boy's life. We have a duty."

******

Jamie dove through the doorway into the dark room, rolling to her feet. The room was empty, as had been the last two. She looked around; Joe was not here. They had been clearing room after room, and so far, Joe was nowhere to be seen. Each room was a perfect square leading through to more of the same. There was an eerie silence, after the crowd in the courtyard. Her team filed in behind her.

******

"Let me tell you our duty, child." Alex was standing, looking down at Joe, who had huddled against a wall. The boy had not given up the fight. Alex could see that. It was a good thing. His children needed to have fight in them. They had to be ready to burn the world. The boy was regrouping as he pretended to be broken. He was sneaky-sneaky, another thing Alex was glad to see. His kids needed to be powerful and sneaky. But they needed to understand. They were close, but so far not yet there. He had run out of time to teach them.

"Camus wrote many great works, not the least being his letters to his German friend. You see, his friend had indicated to Camus that the Germans were better patriots. They did whatever was asked of them. Whatever the country needed, they fulfilled that need. Their duty was to obey. They were, in his opinion, the perfect patriots." Alex walked across the room and stared up at one of the pictures on the wall. Joe leaned back, relieved not to be the center of attention.

"But Camus disagreed. He told the friend that a true patriot was like a parent who loved their child. A bad parent allowed the child to do anything they wanted. The bad parent fed the delusions and bad choices of the child. But a good parent... Well, a good parent loved their child unconditionally while still forcing the child to become the best it could be. They taught the child. They reared the child. They let the child run free, but held the child to a higher standard. They had a duty not just to serve the kingdom, but to shape it. A good patriot was like this. They loved their country but they held it to a higher standard. They demanded the right behavior. They knew their true duty."

Alex pulled the photo from the wall and stared at it as he whispered the last sentence. It was a picture of a young, blonde child in a brilliant white dress. She was smoking a cigarette in a lazy, offhanded fashion. Her long hair trailed wildly around her face and off her shoulders. Her face told the world she was just there for the smoke—the kind of look that meant "I don't care" more than any words could ever capture. Alex had found that those who said the words often cared the most. But those with this look... They were beautiful. The freedom and abandon of the little girl filled the black-and-white image. Alex could stare at this image for years, given the chance. He could hang it over the mantle and look up at it over a drink.

Alex smiled down at the photo before throwing it against the wall. It crashed, glass on wood, in a sharp tinkle of painful memories. Memories came and went; there were too many to hold onto. But the photo had pulled memories from Alex, like dragging the muddy bog of his mind. Bodies, tires, and tin cans all got jumbled on the rope and pulled to the surface. Those memories were his driving force, but he could not focus on them if he wanted to take the next step.

Alex sat next to Joe and sighed a long-tired sigh of regret and powerlessness. He set his jade collar down on the ground between them. This was the child of his teaching, if not his blood. They all were, and they all needed to understand. The children of his teaching must burn the world to free the child of his blood. Blood was vital. It cleansed the world and made the most important connections. This was his legacy, blood. They needed to understand.

"We must demand the same of our cause. Of our goddesses. You kids all think you know the cause you struggle for, but we, at times, must choose between the cause and our duty. The Queen. Uazit. They are not the duty. They are not your master. They are not your family. They are not your duty. I see you, Joe. I see you, and I ask that you hear me, because I have something to teach you."

******

Jamie could see the light under the door and hear the voices slipping softly from underneath. The building had been cleared to this point. She was bloody and ruffled and ready for more. Her body felt electrified. She felt electrified. This night had left her with cuts and bruises along her body and at least one long gash that she thought would need stitches. But she breathed in and felt the joy of it. The joy of the struggle.

Jamie took up a position to the left of the door while Nettle stood to the right. The feeling of anticipation filled her with tension as her body awaited the violence. In a single swift kick, Russ knocked the door clean off its hinges. Jamie could hear it crash against the far wall as María tossed bolts of light in after it. The golden light exploded in the room as Jamie ran in and ducked low, crossing to the right. Nettle came in directly behind her, crossing to the left, sword held high. Russ charged straight in with María behind him in a regal waltz.

Jamie's position to the far right of the room gave her the perfect view of Russ slamming into Joe with the force of a freight train. The hard strike sent shock waves through the broken room, and Jamie could feel the brush of wind across her face.

Joe stood, arm up defensively over his head. Russ' ax bit deeply into that upraised arm, like a tooth sinking into hard bread. Russ' arms bunched as he pressed down against the taller yet thinner man, but Joe did not budge, and his body did not bend. He stood comfortably, considering the eyes of his once good friend. Jamie struck from the right as Nettle swung in from the left. Russ let out a deep huff as he shoved his ax to the left, crashing into Nettle and shearing off the outer layer of Joe's armor.

Jamie struck as Joe struck back. It was not as titanic a collision as the one Russ had forced, but it was a blur of speed. They were striking, dodging, and spinning light—the end of which found Jamie kneeling on the ground, arms up, knives pushing against Joe's downward striking blade. He leaned in over her, pressing harder, forcing her arms to bend back toward her face.

He had a smile on his face.

The golden lightning struck him and threw him back. It filled the air and clawed around him in a violent pummeling of electrical discharge. His arms were up as he attempted to shield his body from the bolts. He seemed to be gritting his teeth as he shoved against the power. It curled and flicked like a hungry tongue along the ivory whiteness of his armor.

Joe seemed to grasp the lightning with his hands and throw it behind him at the now-charging Nettle. The bolts struck Nettle straight on, knocking her back against the wall in a smoke heap of pain. María pulled the bolts back towards her just as Joe struck her with a spiked mace. She fell to the side as he swung into her body over and over in thick, wet crunches. Russ grabbed him by the back of his collar, lifted him away from María's downed form, and slammed him against the floor. Russ lifted him again and slammed him back down. Joe brought one leg up around Russ's arm and twisted in his grip. The loud crack of Russ's arm breaking filled the room as Joe dropped to the floor hard upon his back.

Jamie stood slowly in a ready stance. Joe stood up, shaking, across from her. Without thought, she grasped the moment. María was on the ground to her left, bleeding from wounds that could not be seen from this angle. The long golden mail was ripped and torn in too many places to count. Toward the back of the room, Nettle was likewise down. Her black uniform had burned off across her shoulders and arms, saving her from taking the full brunt of María's strike. She was lying on the ground with a light smoke frozen around her. Russ was up, but his arm hung loosely at his side and his ax lay against the floor. Joe stood frozen and silent. His black hair hung along his face, framing his brown smile. He looked full of power and ready to take on the world. He had grown past the cute boy into a handsome man.

As time reasserted itself, Russ struck out at Joe with his one good arm, only to be knocked back. Jamie dove in, only to be likewise knocked against the closest wall. How had Joe gotten so strong? He had been good, but not good enough to take on the team. What the hell was this? Jamie felt the power fill her as she tried to stand and then slipped back to the ground. Russ was down. He leaned back against a wall, shaking his head, but not in a way that said he would be clearing it soon.

Joe was the image of battle-weary. His white armor was scorched brown and black along the body and arms. Deep cuts and gashes covered its surface, and the entire left arm was sheared through, baring his forearm. Even with the damage, it was easy to see the subtle changes in his overall uniform. It still had a science fiction feel to it, but now it curled around him in a slightly sinister way. The round curves and smooth, shell-like surface were now pockmarked and spiked. Color had bled into the design, and highlights framed his arms and chest. His dark face was open to the air, and he looked older and more confident than he had. He looked tired and happy as he reached out and flipped the golden disc like a coin. "You were my favorite, Jamie. I wanted you to see me more than all the others. I wanted you to see me so that we could see the world together."

"Fuck you, fucking fuck." was Jamie's only response, her eyes upon the coin.

"You do not understand. I see you—you. We are going to burn the world together, I promise. We will be together. We will do our duty."

"Our duty? Our duty is to destroy Order, bring chaos. Look at you—Order's bitch. We will never be together."

A sad look filled Joe's face as he considered her. He shook his head and stepped toward Jamie, towering over her. He raised his hand, and a thick, hard mace of glass formed. His looked sad and as though he might weep as he considered her lying there, trying to get up. He pointed the golden disc at her as if taking aim for his mace. Before he could swing the mace down, a bolt of golden light struck him, knocking him to the side. He tried to turn, but more golden lightning filled the room and covered him, scorching his armor. The power of it forced him to his knees. He struggled, but then began to stand. Jamie could see the golden disc still in his hand, and she dived forward to grab it. As she ripped it out of his hand, Joe began to scream and she rolled to the ground. A thick, black bolt of lightning struck behind him, and from it, Nettle stepped, driving the Raven's Sword deep through his back and out his chest.

The lighting stopped, and Joe and Nettle slipped to the ground. She held him tenderly from behind, like a lover. Like a friend. The illusion was broken as she stood and roughly yanked the sword from his body, which fell limply to the ground. María was up on one leg, leaning against the wall, hand out. Russ stood behind her, holding her up; he must have been there to support her as she threw the lightning. Jamie could barely stand, and the weight of the disc pulled her hand down. She had never felt this tired in her life.

The team was a team, and they proved it as they leaned upon each other, crawling from the building. The blood- and body-packed courtyard was a memory few of them had held onto, but it was a memory that they faced as they exited. The cold night air kissed their faces as they gazed up into the starry sky. Jamie wondered idly, had she stopped the dawn? Would the night keep them in her embrace? If not, how badly would the sun

burn them as it rose?

EPILOGUE

Joe awoke to the cold embrace of a candlelit room. He wore only a thin linen robe that covered his form yet did nothing against the cool air tickling against him. The first things he felt in the darkness were the goose bumps along his skin. They tickled and hurt and forced his eyes open. He whimpered softly before he began to cough. The light of the candles around the room refracted within the hard table he lay upon and reflected upon the walls. It was a copper altar. He attempted to lean forward, and with work found that he could sit up, legs off the table.

The most beautiful woman he had ever seen stood against one wall. She was short and voluptuous, with the most curvaceously attractive form. Her gown seemed to be made of a multitude of thin silk veils layered upon each other and seemed made of ivory and silver when she stood still. Each move she made flared the veils in such a way that Joe was sure he should see skin beneath. But no skin materialized, only colorful beauty through which the outline of flesh could be seen. She smiled at Joe with a cool look. A mother's look. Most importantly, she saw him.

His wounds were gone, but his body was still sore. He tried to stand and felt the robe he wore fall open. In embarrassment, he quickly closed it and wrapped the belt around him. The room he was in looked old. The building was obviously ancient, with the look of medieval gothic that had fallen into disrepair. But the woman, she drew his eyes. A soft, white light shone from her coffee-and-cream-colored skin that illuminated the world around her with a delicate joy. Her long hair reached her knees and was a warm brown with light highlights. The woman was made up of layers upon layers.

"You have come home, Joseph." Her voice was lightly accented, with a taste of Latin at the end of her words. It gave her every phrase a lilt it would not have normally had. The images of her words were beauty she dreamed to existence. Joe could feel the warm embrace of home surround him like a protecting blanket pulled over his head.

"You were dead, now you live. You were in pain, now you feel none. You have learned the most valuable lesson a person can learn in all of life. You learned that all states pass." She looked at him with an air of kindness that filled his heart with glee.

"There is a famous story from ancient times about a king from long ago. They say the King was of Persia. This king was newly minted in his role as master, after taking over from his father. He understood that to rule, he needed wisdom he did not possess. And like all rich men, he decided to pay someone else to do the work. He gathered all the wise folk of his time into one room and asked them to give him that wisdom. His demand was a single phrase that would give him hope in times of loss and drive him to further greatness even in times of plenty. The stories change here. Some say the group came together to create the phrase. Others claim they failed and he sought elsewhere. My favorite is that one old woman came forward with the wisdom required." She laughed gently with a pause, as if to remember days long past.

"All the stories agree, though, that an answer was eventually found. They created a phrase and emblazoned it on a single silver ring they gifted to the king. The phrase was, 'This too shall pass.' The king was skeptical, but he put on the ring and went about his business.

"He became a great king. And as happens to great kings, his neighbors envied his rich and prosperous kingdom, so they attacked it. He went to war." She paused with a smile that warmed Joe's heart. "Well, his troops went to war. In a great battle, he faced insurmountable foes and lost. He hid in the bushes with a few elite soldiers and he despaired. Within his despair, the ring felt heavy on his finger, so he looked upon it and realized that this suffering—this would pass. He had been great, and now he hid in bushes as armies marched on his kingdom. But this failure would pass. He embraced that ideal and rallied his troops. He worked hard to lead them to a great victory against the forces of his enemies and bested them. He conquered city after city. Uniting the very world under him.

"He was faced, then, with how to assimilate these new conquests into his kingdom. Again, the ring weighed upon his finger, and looking at the phrase, he realized this too shall pass. His greatness was not forever. His kingdom was not forever. He had won the day, but what about tomorrow, when his enemies might take what he had won? And so, against the advice of those who told him to annihilate all those who stood against him, he showed compassion. He gave them freedom and a happy life under his rule. He understood that what he held today, he would one day lose. He gave the world Order." Something about the way she spoke sparked memories in Joe of Alex lecturing. But her words shone with an inner light, and Joe felt joy in her presence. He could listen to her talk for hours without growing tired—days, lifetimes. Her light shone outward and embraced him. She saw him.

"If you will be my Champion, you must understand what it is I shall do. I will bring order to this world, Joseph. I will bring order to the gods and spirits of this land. I will bring order to the humans, and they will love me for it. I will remove chaos from this land, and my praises will be sung. I will give to this world the gift of peace and prosperity under one law. And if they resist... if they do not rejoice... they too shall pass."

The white light of righteousness spread from her eyes and voice as she wiped away her imaginary enemies. Joe could feel it, that joy building in him. She was his Queen; they would purge the world. Filled with her righteousness, Joe was capable of pushing himself off the table and standing strong in front of his Queen. His eyes filled bright with fervor. "Yes, my Queen. Yes, we will save the world from monsters."

She laughed at Joe with a bright sprinkling of laughter that filled him with a quiet joy that she could be so happy.

"You do not know, Joseph, what makes us all so special. The children and Chosen of the Tricksters, my Champions. What we call the talking animals and spirits of our world. Have you not realized what makes us different? That saddens my heart, dear child. We are the monsters, each and every one."

Joe leaned back against the table. Even with the joy that filled him, he felt broken.

If you liked this book try the short story of how Hempel came to work with Alex. There is a $.99 version on Amazon, but why buy it when you can download the PDF for free on Dan's blog https://ourorcard.co

And be ready to join Jamie in the next installment of the Tricksters' War series "Raven's Spear"

About the Author

Daniel (known as Dandan) is a philosopher and an artist. He works to become not only an artist but the art that he creates. He is a social philosopher, and has supported his life through helping the casino industry. He is a new author working on his next novel. He has spent his life helping casino's and other businesses achieve higher revenue by providing experience based insight and informed direction through improved analytics and more efficient operations. Dandan started working in gaming in September of 1997 at a tribal casino. He spent his entire adult life managing people. In that work, he found that true success does not come just with a bigger bottom line, but through Servant Leadership. Only by empowering others will one find success in this life. He is nobody, and nothing. Dan has worked his way through the industry by being an objective observer, which allowed him to improve inefficient systems and help people.

Dandan is an enrolled member of the Village of Kotzebue and a voting shareholder of the NANA Corporation. He grew up in rural North Idaho on the Coeur d'Alene Indian Reservation. He has lived in many places, though Honolulu Hawai'i was a favorite. He loves to travel the world and find new places and foods. He loves food, and considers himself a foodie, if a drunken version of one. He is highly eclectic and loves to try new experiences. He lives very much by the doctrine of experience. With recent changes in his life, he has decided to create a blog, "Our Orchard."

Our Orchard will be filled with short stories, book ideas, book promotions, food thoughts, travel enjoyments, and just basic things that come about that Dandan wants to talk about (maybe go over the many ways to make the best cup of coffee, and yes there are many). His goal is not in creating a marketing commercial for his books, but instead create a journal of his adventures.

Dandan has begun a life of traveling and writing. He has become a leaf upon the wind. He spent time at Standing Rock in protest, visited places in the world that sounded illuminating (only continents left to visit (Australia and Antarctica)), and spent a lot of time deciding on what to do next. He has recently decided to live in the enviable (or unenviable as the case maybe) position of being his own master, beholden to none.

In his books and blogs Dandan writes in eclectic and vastly different genres that spiral around each other in a disjointed happiness. He has often failed in life, and through those failures is finding his way to success. He works as a consultant, and may work at another Casino someday. But, he lives his life as a libertine, and an artist of experience.

He is the wind and the wind passes through him. As a hobby and a food source Dandan loves to garden. He even attempted to create a gardening app a while back on

<u>Kickstarter</u>. He loves the warm sun on his face and the dirt in his hands. Spring in Idaho is the perfect time to live in the now. Dandan has learned through his years of gardening that to expect flowers one must plant seeds.

Personal Note

It is my goal to learn how to best sow the future I wish to have. I seek to learn the best way to live in this world, and I plan on sharing that journey. I invite you to join me on my adventure. The time has come to embrace the next step in life. To find a better way to enjoy my world. Follow me as together we plant seeds and grow our orchard

Visit Daniel Hansen at:

Blog

https://ourorchard.co/

LinkedIn

https://www.linkedin.com/in/daniel-hansen-032900b3

Twitter

https://twitter.com/DandanHansen?lang=en

Author Central

https://amazon.com/author/dandanhansen

Facebook

https://www.facebook.com/dandan.hansen

Minds

https://www.minds.com/dandanhansen

Instagram

https://www.instagram.com/dhansen541/?hl=en

Made in the USA
Lexington, KY
26 April 2017